Nashv...

The midwi... ...le City!

Welcome to Nashville, Tennessee! The home of
country music *and* Skylar, Brianna and Lori.
Midwives at Legacy Women's Clinic, they dedicate
their days and nights to their patients. But when
Skylar, Brianna and Lori aren't helping to bring
bundles of joy into the world, they are facing meet-
cutes with colleagues that leave hearts racing!
Will their love stories be so magical they could
inspire the city's next big country star as they sing
their latest hit on the Bluebird Café's stage...?

Find out in...

Skylar and Jared's story
Unbuttoning the Bachelor Doc
Available now!

And don't miss...

Brianna and Knox's story
and
Lori and Zac's story

Coming soon!

Dear Reader,

Welcome to Nashville's Legacy Women's Clinic, where the doctors and midwives always work together to make every patient feel like a VIP, including some of country music's biggest stars.

I love the city of Nashville, Tennessee. It has an energy that is like no other. Home of the Grand Ole Opry and local downtown bars where you can hear young musicians perform day and night, it's no wonder that it has become known as Music City. So when I decided to base my next three books on a trio of midwives, I knew I had to include the country music scene in their stories.

So put your best country duds on and have a great time as Sky and Jared find their lives suddenly filled with country music stars, glamorous parties and, most importantly, the magic of that first kiss.

And as Sky would say, "Don't forget to have fun along the way."

Deanne Anders

UNBUTTONING THE BACHELOR DOC

DEANNE ANDERS

Harlequin

MEDICAL ROMANCE

Harlequin®
MEDICAL
ROMANCE

Recycling programs
for this product may
not exist in your area.

ISBN-13: 978-1-335-59547-8

Unbuttoning the Bachelor Doc

Copyright © 2024 by Denise Chavers

Harlequin Enterprises ULC
22 Adelaide St. West, 41st Floor
Toronto, Ontario M5H 4E3, Canada
www.Harlequin.com

Printed in U.S.A.

Deanne Anders was reading romance while her friends were still reading Nancy Drew, and she knew she'd hit the jackpot when she found a shelf of Harlequin Presents in her local library. Years later she discovered the fun of writing her own. Deanne lives in Florida with her husband and their spoiled Pomeranian. During the day she works as a nursing supervisor. With her love of everything medical and romance, writing for Harlequin Medical Romance is a dream come true.

Books by Deanne Anders

Harlequin Medical Romance

From Midwife to Mommy
The Surgeon's Baby Bombshell
Stolen Kiss with the Single Mom
Sarah and the Single Dad
The Neurosurgeon's Unexpected Family
December Reunion in Central Park
Florida Fling with the Single Dad
Pregnant with the Secret Prince's Babies
Flight Nurse's Florida Fairy Tale
A Surgeon's Christmas Baby

Visit the Author Profile page at Harlequin.com.

This book is dedicated to Beth Diamond, one of the most dedicated and caring L&D nurses that I ever had the privilege of working with. Small in stature she might have been, but she was mighty in her love for God, her family and her friends.

**Praise for
Deanne Anders**

"This story captivated me. I enjoyed every moment [of] it. This is a great example of a medical romance. Deanne Anders is an amazing writer!"
—*Goodreads* on *The Surgeon's Baby Bombshell*

CHAPTER ONE

SKYLAR BENTON HURRIED to the last seat available around the large conference table. It was the first Thursday of the month and she wasn't surprised to find the room crowded. Everyone who worked at Legacy Women's Clinic, from the medical assistants to the four physicians employed at the practice, wanted to be present for their monthly meeting. Lori, one of the other midwives, believed that it was the dedication of the staff that was responsible for their attendance. While Sky wouldn't argue that they had one of the most dedicated OB-GYN offices in Nashville, she was pretty sure that it was the dozens of hot, delicious doughnuts that their office manager, Tanya, brought in for the meeting that was the true draw.

"You look rough. Didn't you get any sleep last night?" Lori asked from beside her.

"Thanks a lot. I'll be sure to remind you how awful you look next time you have to pull an all-nighter." Not that it would be true. Her friend couldn't look bad if she tried to.

"It's just all part of the glamorous life of a midwife," Lori said, bumping her shoulder against Sky's.

Sky didn't feel very glamorous, sitting there in rumpled scrubs that she'd worn for the last twenty-four hours. It was great having a thriving midwifery practice, but it wasn't the same as an obstetrician's. A midwife worked with their patient for hours before the birth, sometimes acting not only as the provider of care but also in some ways as a doula who provided more hands-on support through the labor process. That was how she'd spent all of last night with three of her patients that were in labor.

And she still had one more delivery to do before she could go home and crash. Unfortunately, it was her patient's first baby and things weren't progressing as quickly as either one of them would like.

The smell of freshly baked doughnuts drifted down the length of the table as one of the boxes came closer. Her hand reached for the soft, glazed pastry before her brain could scold her on the lack of nutrients in her vice of choice. Closing her eyes, she embraced the rush of sugar as the doughnut all but melted in her mouth. Holding back a moan as she licked the sticky sweetness off her lips, she opened her eyes and froze. Across the table, dark brown eyes met hers and held. How had she not noticed him when she sat down? Refusing to be the first one to look away, Sky took another bite and chewed slowly while she tried to figure out what was going on. Dr. Jared Warner usually made a point of avoiding her, just as she did her best to get his attention. It had turned into a game of sorts between the two of them. One she had begun to actually enjoy.

Unable to help herself, she licked her lips again. Jared's eyes darted down as she made a point of dragging her tongue all the way around her mouth. His eyes met hers once more before he looked away.

"Chicken," Sky said, too soft for the man to hear her.

"What?" Lori asked.

"Nothing," Sky said, suddenly remembering where she was. Glancing around the room she was relieved to see that no one had been watching as she'd done her best to rock her stone-cold coworker.

Of course, she normally was more aware of her surroundings and made sure not to get caught teasing him, and she'd never gone this far with her teasing. He was just so much of a stick-in-the-mud, never wanting to step out of his well-beaten, boring path. He was always work, then more work. He didn't joke. He didn't tease. He never wanted to play. He was missing all the fun there was to have in life. Why that irritated her so much, she didn't know. Maybe it was because she saw herself, the person she'd been before she'd came to Nashville, in him. Or maybe it was because of the first time she'd seen him smile in a delivery. Picturing him with that big grin on his face, holding that screaming baby, still warmed her heart. It had been so natural. And so unexpected from a man who had always hid his emotions from not only her but everyone around them. After that, watching him return to that stony, totally boring exterior, she'd decided to make it her job to crack him open and see what was really inside. And so had begun her game of "shock the doc."

There were times when she just couldn't keep herself from ruffling his feathers with some silent nonsensical gestures. What was the harm? She'd even caught him smiling a few times when she'd flashed him a silly face. So what if she made herself look foolish. He had a really nice smile and it was a pity that he didn't let people see it more. Still, he was her boss's son, and she didn't want to ever disappoint the senior Dr. Warner with behavior he might not approve of, so it wasn't something she would normally do in a crowded room of her coworkers.

As Sky tried to concentrate on finishing her doughnut, making sure to keep her eyes to herself now, the door to the conference room opened and the elder Dr. Warner rushed in. With his silver hair combed back and his kind baby blue eyes, he looked like someone's favorite grandpa. "Good morning, everyone. I hope you are all doing well on this beautiful spring morning."

He took his seat at the front of the table and Tanya handed him a tablet. "Thank you, Tanya, I know each of you has a busy day today, so let's get started. First off, I'd like to welcome two new colleagues. I hope you've all met our new resident midwife, Brianna Rogers. She's a recent graduate of Vanderbilt and came to us highly recommended."

"Go Commodores," yelled one of the med techs from the other side of the table.

Everyone laughed at the man's shout-out for Nashville's largest university, which the majority of the staff had attended. Sky waved down the table at the young woman that had joined the practice a few days earlier. While Lori would be Brianna's primary preceptor, there would be times when Sky would be helping, and secretly Sky was hoping Brianna would stay after her residency was done. Their practice was growing, and it would be nice to have a third midwife on staff.

"Also, I want you to welcome Dr. Knox Collins, who will be filling in for Dr. Hennison, who, I'm sure you all know, just welcomed another baby boy."

As Dr. Warner began going through the monthly budget, Sky nudged Lori's arm and shot a sideways glance at the dangerously hot man sitting to Dr. Warner's left. How was it possible that she had missed seeing him? It had been all the office had talked about since they'd discovered that Nashville's own bad-boy doctor was going to be their new ad locum doc. With both his parents legendary country music stars, Knox had been covered by all the local media growing up. Sky just hoped that once it got out that he had returned home the media would not be hounding the office.

"And lastly, I'd like to share with you a special opportunity that has just become available to the practice." Dr. Warner handed the tablet back to the office manager and looked around the table, stopping when his eyes met Sky's. "It seems one of our midwives has been highly recommended to one of Nashville's rising stars. As most of Nashville is aware, Mindy and Trey Carter have recently relocated here from Chattanooga and are expecting their first child in just three months."

"They're the ones with the reality show, right?" asked the medical assistant sitting next to Sky.

"I've seen that show," Tanya said. "Cute couple and very talented."

Sky knew of the couple too. They'd made big news when their debut album had hit record sale numbers. With their reality show beginning to air, there probably wasn't a single person in Music City that hadn't heard of the young couple.

"I've met them personally and they are a lovely couple that are very excited about the birth of their first child. Both Mindy and her husband plan to be very involved. Of course, as always, everyone will be expected to keep our patients' information private. Also, as an added bonus, the couple has requested that their midwife and doctor be involved to a certain point with their new show."

Everyone around the table started talking at once, some excited about the prospect and some of the staff shocked by the request. Their practice had cared for high-profile patients before, including famous musicians, but this was different. This was big and exciting.

"Yes, yes… I know this is an unusual request, but it comes with a very large donation to Legacy House," the senior Dr. Warner said, silencing everyone in the room. Legacy House was the home for pregnant women in need that Dr. Warner had established not long after he'd opened the Legacy Clinic after seeing that some of his younger patients didn't have the support at home that they needed during their pregnancy and postdelivery. While the home depended mainly on donations, everyone in their office played a part in supporting it with their time and talents, doing everything from tutoring to home repairs. Still, Sky knew the home provided care for a lot of women and it wasn't unusual for their budget to run short some months. Sky had always suspected that Dr. Warner personally covered those months. She also suspected it was one of the reasons the doctor was still practicing instead of retiring, or at least cutting back on his hours, as other doctors his age often did.

"So, as you can see, this is an opportunity that we are lucky to be able to accept. *If* we accept. As always, we all need to remember to keep our patients' information private." Dr. Warner stood, signaling that their meeting was over. "Thank y'all for coming today. Jared and Sky, can the two of you give me a few more minutes, please?"

Jared looked from his father to Sky. He wasn't sure what his father was up to, but from the meeting he had an idea. A really bad idea that included the midwife sitting across from him. The same midwife who only a few minutes earlier had made him squirm in his seat. The same one who seemed to love to annoy him. The same one who enjoyed playing silly games instead of taking life seriously.

"Isn't this exciting?" his dad asked as he walked over and took a seat next to Jared, his eyes dancing with a joy for life Jared had never understood, considering all the man had been through, with the loss of a child and then later his wife.

Exciting? It was more like a nightmare. "Maybe you should tell us exactly what the plan is. I take it that the three of us are going to have something to do with this new VIP patient and her husband?"

"I'm so glad that you are ready to jump in here to help, Jared. I knew I could count on you and Sky," his father said. With anyone else, Jared would have thought he was being sarcastic. But not his father. No, Dr. Jack Warner didn't do sarcasm. He always chose to see the best in others. It was part of his charm and sometimes it made Jared wish he was truly his father's son. Maybe then he'd be able to relate to his father's optimistic nature.

But after spending two years of his life in and out of foster homes, Jared's eyes had been permanently opened to what really went on in the world. There were no rose-colored glasses in his life.

"Excuse me, Dr. Warner," Sky said, "I'm sorry to interrupt, but I need to get back over to the hospital. I have a primigravida that has been laboring for several hours."

"How many hours? Has her water broken?" Jared asked. The risk of infection increased significantly during prolonged rupture of membranes.

"Her water broke spontaneously at four centimeters, only four hours ago. She's afebrile and the baby's heart tones are fine. Anything else,

Doctor?" The fire in Sky's eyes warned him that she was ready to ignite, something Jared didn't appreciate. Even though Sky worked independently, if something went wrong and her patient required a cesarean section, it would become his responsibility. His questions had been appropriate.

"Just keep me updated. I took over call at seven and I will start making rounds as soon as we are done here."

"Okay, then," Jared's father said, plainly trying to act as peacekeeper, "let's get on with it. I met with Mindy and Trey yesterday, along with their manager, and they are all very nice people. I think working with them will be a pleasure." His dad looked across the table. "Sky, it seems that you took care of one of Mindy's band members, Jenny Mack, during her pregnancy and delivery a few years ago and she has, almost literally according to Mindy, sung your praises to her boss."

"I remember her. She had to schedule her appointments around rehearsal and gig dates. I don't think she was with the Carters then."

It always amazed Jared how Sky could remember her patients so clearly. He tried to remember his patients' names, but between his obstetrics practice and the gyn surgeries he performed, he found it impossible unless something really stood out about the patient. It wasn't how he had planned his career, but it was what it was. He was doing his best to build a practice and hopefully take over for his father someday. He had to see as many patients as possible, which sometimes limited their interaction more than he would like.

"Well, she seems to remember you too, and Mindy is very excited about meeting you. She is determined to have a midwifery delivery. Her husband, on the other hand, has some concerns. That's where you come in, Jared. In order to give this young couple the delivery they both want, I'm going to need the two of you to work closely together."

"What exactly do you need me to do?" Jared asked. He definitely wasn't one to discourage an expectant father from having a doctor oversee the birth of his child.

"I need the two of you to work as a team. This couple has a lot of pressure on them right now. They're new to the superstar level of country music and from what I can tell, the reality show is causing some…shall we say *stress* on the two of them. It's not good for either one of them, especially Mindy and the baby. Her last pregnancy ended in a miscarriage at nineteen weeks." Turning to him, his father looked him in the eye. "I know I can trust the two of you to do what is best for this couple and work together as the professional colleagues that you are."

Jared glanced at his dad and then over to Sky, who had gone unusually quiet. There were dark rings under her eyes and strands of blond hair hung loose around her face where it had come out of the band she kept it tied up in. He hadn't noticed that this morning. It had been all he could do to keep himself on his side of the table when all he'd wanted to do was lick that sticky sugar off those luscious lips of hers.

"What about the reality show? Do they really expect us to be part of that?" she asked, and Jared wasn't surprised to see a flicker of excitement in her tired eyes. She was the outgoing, flashy type of person they usually had on those kinds of shows. Not that he had any intention on being on the show himself. He didn't care for all that "reality" drama. He'd had enough drama as a child. Just the thought sent shivers through him.

"From what I can gather, you would only be there on the sidelines as you interact with them as providers for the pregnancy," his father said. "And don't forget what this will mean for

Legacy House. Things are tough financially for a lot of people right now. Some of our regular donors have had to cut back on their giving. This donation would cover the rest of this year's budget. And then there's the possibility that they will tell others about the work Legacy House does. The two of you might even have an opportunity to tell others about it."

Sky's phone vibrated with a message, and she got up from the table as she read it. "I need to get back to the hospital."

She reached for the last doughnut left on the table before standing and heading to the door, then she stopped and looked back at his father. "Is it really that bad, Jack?"

The reassuring smile that was as much a part of his father as breathing faltered. "It's not just the lack of regular donations that's straining our budget. A lot of people are struggling right now, which means more young girls are coming to us for help. We are close to having to turn them away for the first time in twenty years."

Sky's eyes locked on Jared, then narrowed. Her chin went up and he felt like one of those unfortunate ants caught under a magnifying glass about to be zapped. "Whatever they need us to do, we're in, aren't we, Jared?"

Jared's mouth dropped open to argue, but then he shut it. How could he get out of this without looking like a jerk? It wasn't that he didn't want to help Legacy House. He'd been helping out at the home since he was a teenager. But working with this free-spirited midwife who acted like life was just another game would be a disaster. Look at how she'd resented him asking basic questions about her patients. How could they coordinate their care of their patient if she reacted that way every time he asked a question?

And then there was her unprofessional teasing of him. Those big warm smiles and sassy winks rattled him. How much worse would it be if he had to work even closer with her?

Without waiting for his agreement, she spun around and headed for the door, the doughnut still in her hand.

"Well, I'm glad that's settled," his dad said, taking off his glasses and laying them down on the table.

"Why me?" Jared asked. "You know I'm not good at all that schmoozing with people. Wouldn't it make more sense for you to do this? Wouldn't the husband feel better having someone with your experience?"

"You're fine with people when you want to

be. You just hold yourself back. You need to relax more. You're thirty-six years old. It's time you get out in the world and experience life instead of spending all your time working."

"You're one to talk. You've been going strong for almost forty years now. If anyone needs to slow down, it's you."

"When I was your age, I was married and building a home for me and Katie. The years we had together were the best years of my life. And when you came into our life you made us the family we always wanted to be. I want that for you, what I had with your mom, because no matter what you think right now, there will come a time when you'll need someone. Someone that understands you and will be by you no matter what happens."

His father suddenly looked ten years older than he had when he'd been rallying the troops at their monthly meeting. Was it the memory that he'd once had a family that didn't include Jared? Was it the memory of the little girl he'd lost? Jared knew he'd never taken the little girl's place in his parents' hearts. Not that he had wanted to. The Warners had been good to him and had treated him like their own. He had no resentment of their daughter, though at times he knew he'd disappointed them by not being able to be the outgoing, happy child they'd deserved. Maybe if in his younger years he'd been surrounded by the secure love they'd always given him, things would have been different. Maybe he would have been different. But that wasn't his reality. The life he'd lived being raised by a sickly grandmother and then later in foster homes had made him who he was. He couldn't change his past.

But it wasn't the time for them to get into an old argument that he knew he wasn't going to win. Jared lived his life just like he liked it: drama free. He worked hard and in his off time enjoyed the peace and quiet of the home he'd built for himself. He didn't need anyone else in his life. And he certainly didn't want to ever rely on another person for his happiness. Everyone he'd relied on as a child had left him or sent him away. By the time he'd been adopted by Jack and Katie, he'd learned his lesson. Not that he didn't care for them. They had been the best thing that had ever happened to him.

"But back to the Carters. You're overthinking this, Jared. I have full confidence in both your and Sky's professionalism. I know the two of you will make a great team."

He could see he wasn't going to get out of this. His dad had made up his mind. As Nana

Marie used to tell him when he had to do something he didn't want to do, *Boy, put on your big boy pants and get it done.*

And so it was time for him to accept the inevitable and make the best of the situation. His only hope of getting out of this would be for Sky to refuse to work with him, and he couldn't count on that. Still, it wouldn't hurt to talk to her. Unlike his father, she would see that the two of them working together could only lead to disaster. He just had to find a way to get her to agree with him.

CHAPTER TWO

"YOU'RE DOING GREAT," Sky said as she wiped Liza's forehead with a cool rag.

"No, I'm not. I'm so tired. And I gave in and got an epidural after I swore I wouldn't need one. My sister is never going to let me live it down," Liza said.

"Well, I'm not telling her," Sky said, then looked pointedly at the young man at her patient's side. Waiting for him to take the hint was almost painful. Liza's husband almost looked as bad as she did. "No one will ever know, will they, Eric?"

"Oh, no, no…of course not," Eric said.

Liza looked over at him, disbelieving. "You're going to keep a secret? You are the worst blabbermouth in the whole family."

Eric shrugged his shoulders and looked up at Sky from the chair at his wife's bedside with a look of guilt that belonged more on a five-year-old child's face than that of a grown man. Sky looked away before Liza could see her grin.

"The most important thing is that you're fully dilated now. We could start pushing, or we could turn you over on your side and let you rest for half an hour." Sky was hoping that Liza would choose to rest a while. The baby hadn't progressed down as much as she'd like before they started pushing. Sky was tired and she knew Liza was even more tired at this point. The two of them could both use a power nap while the contractions did their own magic of bringing the baby down lower.

"Is that okay to do? Won't the baby's head end up funny shaped?" Eric asked.

"It's perfectly fine. Your baby's head has to mold as it comes down the birthing canal. That's why baby's heads sometimes look funny when they're born, but they don't stay that way." Sky found the things that new dads worried about amusing.

"And Baby Stella's heart tones are perfect. It will give the baby some time to move down now that Liza is relaxed, and a little rest will help when she's ready to push." Sky was a strong advocate of letting the patient's body tell them when it was time to push unless there was concern for getting the baby out quickly.

"I'd like to rest a bit, if it's okay," Liza said.

Tammy, the labor and delivery nurse, came into the room and they discussed their plan to give Liza a break. After positioning Liza on her left side to rest, Sky lowered the lights in the room and stepped outside.

"Dr. Warner was looking for you," Tammy said, then clarified, "the young one."

So much for a power nap. Sky reached down deep and tried to find the patience she would need to deal with Jared in the moods they both were in. She was tired, and he was aggravated about being forced to work with her. If she hadn't been so tired, she would have looked forward to their interaction. She'd enjoyed placing him in a situation where he couldn't refuse the opportunity his father had given them. Seeing the uptight doc squirm was always entertaining. He was so cute when he was flustered. And those rare times when she made him smile, those she treasured.

But that wouldn't be the reason Jared had followed her straight over to the unit. He'd said he was on call, and he always rounded on the patients he was covering whether they were his patients or one of the midwives' patients. But while Dr. Hennison and the senior Dr. Warner usually just checked in with her or Lori, trusting them to share if there were any concerns or complications with their patient, Jared took it a couple steps further. He made it a habit to check the midwife patient's medical records and ask questions of the nurses taking care of them, as if Sky was withholding some information from him.

She had never understood why Lori wasn't bothered by this as much as Sky was. The relationship between the doctors and midwives in their practice was a collaboration and she believed sometimes Jared came close to crossing the line. Of course, as there was an understanding that if there were complications in the labor process the practice's doctors would assume care for any necessary procedures, such as surgery, it could be said that Jared's level of interest was reasonable. But still, all of his questioning made her feel as if he didn't believe midwives were equal partners in the practice. There was even a rumor that he had tried to talk his father out of hiring midwives into the practice, and it made her more than a little bit defensive when she had to deal with him, just like she had been earlier that morning when he'd questioned her in front of his father.

"Tammy told me that your patient was complete. Why isn't she pushing?" Jared asked the moment she took a seat in the nurses' station.

Sky looked at Tammy, who cast an apologetic smile her way. There was something about Jared, even though he could be as prickly as a porcupine, that made the staff trust him. Maybe it was the way he always had their backs when the staff was negotiating with the hospital administration. Or maybe it was the fact that Jared never left the staff to handle a difficult patient on their own. Or maybe it was simply that he didn't talk down to them, instead he respected them for the job they did.

If only Sky could get him to respect the midwives the same way. If only he could see that they had a place in the delivery room just as much as he did. There was a story there, and someday she would find out what it was.

"Liza just got an epidural and has chosen to rest a few minutes before we begin pushing." Sky wouldn't let him make her second-guess herself. She had done this hundreds of times. "As you can see on the monitor, the baby's heart tones have good variability along with accelerations."

"See, this is why we can't work together. You resent every question I ask," Jared said, turning toward her, his voice too intense for her lack of sleep.

Sky looked at him and blinked. Was this about her patient or was this about them teaming up to care for Mindy Carter? "I guess you couldn't talk your dad into taking over the Carters' case?"

His eyes refused to acknowledge that she'd seen right through him. His lips straightened into a flat line, but not before she saw him grimace. She'd seen it many times when she'd tried to get a rise out of him. It was as if the man was trying to convince her that he was above having human emotions. But she knew better. She'd seen the way his eyes had watched her lips that morning in their meeting. Was it possible that Jared was as curious about her as she was about him? Was there even the possibility that he was more than curious? Was the way he watched her this morning a sign that he might be interested in her in other ways?

Or maybe not. Maybe it was just her that felt that electric buzz that seemed to arc between the two of them. The only time she ever got any type of response from Jared himself was when they were playing one of their silent games, which just mostly seemed to annoy him. This morning could have been nothing more serious than the man was hungry.

"I simply voiced my belief that it would be better for my father to be the one that represented the practice with such a high-profile case. Don't you agree?"

The truth was she did agree with Jared. Even though she enjoyed her game of irritating him, the two of them had never worked well together. She resented his overpowering need to meddle, and he didn't trust her. It would probably be a nightmare, but she still understood why the senior Dr. Warner wanted his son to be the one to take the lead in this collaboration. It was a known fact that Jared was being mentored by his father to take over the practice someday. It was better to find out now if Jared could take the pressure that was sure to go along with the job.

"I respect your father enough to believe he knows what he is doing," she replied, though she did wonder if she was the right midwife for this job even though she had been highly recommended. The Carters had become unbelievably famous and certainly more well-to-do, as her grandmother would have called them. Sky had been raised in a simple two-bedroom house along with her six siblings and her grandmother in Tennessee's rural mountains. She'd had little to no training on how to behave with people like the Carters.

"Look, Jared, your father has made his decision, and for the sake of the practice and for Legacy House, we have to go through with this no matter how much you don't like me." There. Now the real problem was on the table for the two of them to address. The only way to deal with this was head-on. If the two of them couldn't be friends, the least they could do was learn to work together. Otherwise it was going to be a miserable three months.

"I didn't say I didn't like you. This has nothing to do with how I feel about you." Jared's brows crinkled with confusion. "I don't even know you that well."

"And we've worked together for over three years. Doesn't that seem a little strange to you?" The wrinkles in his forehead got deeper as he stared at her. Was he really this disconnected from all the staff? Or was it just her?

"I know you are a good midwife," Jared said, which coming from him was a huge compliment. Maybe there was hope for them after all.

"And I know you are a very thorough doctor." She'd had her patients' records combed through by him so many times that there was no doubt of that. "So let's start there and maybe by the time this is over we will both have learned more about each other."

His forehead relaxed, but his eyes narrowed as if he suspected that he was being tricked somehow. Maybe it hadn't been such a good idea teasing him so much in the conference room this morning. But it had been fun, and she figured fun was something Jared could use more of in his life. And what could be more fun, or more disastrous, than being on a reality show together with a couple of country music stars?

"How about we go to the first meeting with Mindy and Trey and their manager and see how it goes? It might be that once they meet us they decide we're not a good fit for them. Will you at least agree to that?" Sky looked over to the monitor displaying the laboring patient's fetal heart tones. Liza's tracing was beginning to show signs of head compression, a sure sign that the baby was progressing down into the birth canal.

"I've got to get back to my patient," she said as she stood to leave. "Let me know what you decide. Instead of looking at this as a form of punishment, maybe we should look at this as a great way to do something different and unique. Who knows, you might find that you like being in the spotlight. It might even be fun."

Without waiting for him to give her an answer, she walked out and headed to her patient's room. Somewhere in her pep talk she'd found herself getting excited about working with the music stars despite having to work with Jared. At least she told herself that it was the hobnobbing with the rich and famous that excited—and scared—her. She didn't want to admit that she hoped she might finally tear open that cold box Dr. Jared Warner hid inside of.

And who knew? Maybe she'd find the man wasn't made out of ice. Maybe she'd find the man was just waiting for a chance to come out and play.

CHAPTER THREE

JARED HAD KNOWN this was a mistake the moment Sky had gotten into his truck. They were both headed to the same place, so it had only made sense for the two of them to share the ride. But once the car door had shut, he'd been at a loss for what to say to the one person he'd done his best to avoid since she'd come to work at the practice.

There had always been an awkwardness between the two of them. It was something he didn't want to examine, because it might lead to a more uncomfortable problem. Awkwardness he could handle, but sometimes this felt more…personal. As if something unsaid between them,which made it very important that he avoid her as much as possible. Of course, that wasn't how Sky approached him at all. She was always pulling one of her silent pranks, flirting with him like she'd done at the last staff meeting or winking at him across a nurses' station when no one was looking, all of which he knew she did just to make him uncomfortable. It was those times when he wondered exactly what her intention was. It was like she was just having fun with him, while he was squirming with adult responses that he had no right to be feeling for a coworker. Not that she was acting that way this morning. No, there was none of her usual cheekiness. None of her teasing or her laughter. This morning she was so subdued that he worried she might be sick.

Not that he was complaining. The last thing he needed was to walk into a room with their new patient and have Sky pull one of her stunts, throwing him off his game.

The morning traffic had been heavy as the Nashville workforce started their day. They had been on the road for almost thirty minutes by the time they left Nashville and headed out of town on I-24 toward Clarksville to the ranch where the Carters had recently relocated. He'd spent his time concentrating on getting them safely through the snarl of traffic, but now that they had left the city, the silence surrounding them was deafening. He needed to say something, but he didn't know what. He wasn't a casual conversationalist. He spoke when he needed to. He greeted the office and hospital staff every day. Sometimes he even joined in on the Monday morning college football debate. He even knew which staff members to avoid if Vanderbilt had lost their Saturday game.

But this one-on-one stuff? He wasn't good at it. And, like so many other things in his life, he had learned to avoid it.

"Have you ever met anyone famous?" Sky asked. Even though her question came from out of the blue, he was glad that one of them had finally broken the silence.

"I operated on the mayor's wife a few years ago," he said, though he'd be more likely to recognize the tumor he had removed from her than to recognize the woman, even if her picture was plastered on a roadside billboard.

"Hmm," Sky said. He glanced over to see her staring down at her hands. Her top lip was poked out and she was chewing on her bottom one. Seeing this vulnerable side of Sky bothered him. He was used to feeling out of place. Being shuffled from foster home to foster home after his grandmother's death, he'd never felt that there was a place for him. Even now, after being adopted by the kindest couple in the state of Tennessee, he still didn't know where he belonged. It was like something was off with him but he couldn't put his finger on what it was, nor could he figure out how to correct it.

"Nervous about meeting the Carters?" he asked, though that didn't make sense. She was always so confident.

And why was he suddenly so worried about Sky and her feelings? He didn't do feelings. Feelings just complicated things. It was just another sign that this plan of his father's for them to work together was doomed.

"I just don't want to embarrass the practice," Sky said, before turning toward the window.

"I'm sure they put their cowboy boots on the same way everyone else does," he said as he followed his car's GPS instructions and took the next exit.

"Maybe," she said, still sounding nothing like the midwife he was used to dealing with.

"What's wrong? I thought you were excited about this," Jared said, though he told himself he needed to stop with the questioning. He had already passed the point of casual conversation.

"I am, kind of. I just don't know what to expect. What if they're not the nice couple everybody says they are? What if they're really stuck-up? What if they don't like me?"

"Why would you think that?" Was it possible that the flamboyantly outgoing Sky was having some type of confidence crisis? "Your patients always love you. That's why we're here today."

"I'm being silly. Of course they'll like me," she said before letting out an exaggerated sigh. Jared wasn't sure if she was trying to convince him or herself.

Then she sat up straighter and seemed to relax as she continued to stare out at where the cityscape had turned to open fields. "Oh, isn't this pretty? It's hard to believe we're only a few miles from the city."

Jared took his own deep breath, relieved that she'd moved on from all her misgivings. He had enough of his own to worry about.

"This must be it," she said, straining her neck to see the sign stating they had arrived at The Midnight Ranch. A plain dirt road ran between two fenced-in fields, then disappeared around a curve of trees. "Look, they have horses."

Three horses, one black and two a rusty brown, stopped their grazing and watched the car as it passed. Sky turned around in her seat to admire them, her body almost vibrating with excitement. This was more like the Sky he was used to dealing with.

"I've always thought that horses live a great life. Just look at the three of them. Wouldn't it be nice to have the freedom they have?" Sky asked.

"I guess they have a good life. Most are fed and cared for. Of course, they're really not that free. It's not like they are let loose to roam. They have to stay behind a fence." Jared had never given a horse's life much thought, but Sky was probably right—if their owners cared for them, they had a pretty safe life.

"I hadn't thought about that. I wonder if they resent looking over the railing at the pasture next door and not being able to get to it," Sky said, turning back around in her seat.

Jared hadn't meant to take away her enjoyment of seeing the horses. "We all have to live with boundaries."

"But most of the time, at least when we are adults, we set our own boundaries," Sky said, her voice dropping to almost a whisper. "I think that's worse than having others do that to us."

The pain in Sky's voice surprised him. If anyone lived life without boundaries, it was her.

A few yards farther down the winding drive they came to a wrought iron gate.

"Smile for the camera," Jared said as he

rolled down the truck's window to punch in the code the Carters' manager had emailed to him.

Before he could stop her, Sky undid her seat belt and crawled over the truck console, her body brushing against his as she leaned out of his window. She was almost sitting in his lap and his body reacted immediately, his arms coming around her waist to keep her from falling out onto the road. The smile she gave the camera was one of her one-thousand-watt smiles. It was the same smile she would send him across the nurses' station that he knew she gave him to make him uncomfortable. It was a smile so beautiful that it took his breath away. His body hardened under her, and his arms tightened around her on instinct. "Don't you think you should at least wait for the reality show before you start performing?"

"I was just having a bit of fun? Maybe you should try it before you start criticizing me. You might find you like it," she said as she moved back into her seat, his arms falling away from her and his body suddenly cold without the warmth of hers.

He'd regretted the words the moment he'd said them. She was right. She was just being her normal self. It wasn't her fault that he'd responded to her the way he had. He straightened in his seat, refusing to let himself dwell on that unwanted need he'd felt to close his arms around her. It didn't make sense. It was almost laughable.

And laugh was what she'd do if she knew just what having his hands on her had done to him. Halfway around the next curve, he was glad to see the house come into view. He needed to get out of the truck and put some distance between the two of them.

It was two stories with an outside balcony running the length of the top floor. With large cedar posts and a front porch that ran the length of the house, Jared could tell that the architect had tried to create the look of a simple country home, but the size of the house made that almost impossible. Just the grandeur of the tall, double-glass front doors spoke of luxury that was way out of Jared's price range.

"Wow," Sky said, her voice low as if someone might be listening. "If my grandmamma could just see this."

Jared didn't know anything about Sky's grandmother, but he knew his own grandmother would never believe that he had been invited to a house this grand. Still, he'd give anything to have been driving Nana Marie up to this big house. Just to be able to show her that he'd done it. He'd made something of his life. Not that this represented his life... His life was more simple, quiet and safe. But most of all, *his*. He'd never have to worry about someone taking his home away from him. And that was the most important thing to him.

But still, his nana would have enjoyed this. All of this. She'd followed all the country music stars when she'd been alive, yet she'd never met one, even though a lot of them lived just minutes away from her. She was too busy working and raising him. Then she'd been too sick to leave the house, but somehow she'd still taken care of him. He'd once told her that when he was grown and rich he'd buy her the nicest house in Nashville. His five-year-old brain hadn't even known someplace like this existed.

As his truck came to a stop behind a black SUV parked in the circular drive, a woman whose gray hair was piled as high as the heels she was wearing rushed down the front porch stairs toward them. With bright red lipstick that matched her suit, she marched toward them with an intensity that made Jared want to put the truck in Reverse and speed back down the road toward town.

"Who do you think that is?" Sky asked,

showing no signs of being intimidated by the woman.

"A fire-breathing dragon?" Jared questioned as he unbuckled his seat belt and opened the door.

Sky looked over at him and laughed as she undid her own buckle. Her eyes danced with the humor she was known for. "Don't worry. If she starts spitting fire I'll protect you."

He was pleased to see that she was back to her normal ridiculousness after recovering from her earlier dip in confidence—which didn't make sense, as he'd always found this flirty, flippant side of her irritating.

Before the two of them could make it around to the front of the truck, the woman in red bore down on them, waving a stack of papers in their faces. "I need your signatures on these nondisclosure forms before I can allow you inside."

"Marjorie, can you at least let them come inside before you start hounding them with all that privacy nonsense?" a young woman called after her.

Jared looked up to the front door, where a young woman, no more than twenty-five or -six, stood with her arms resting on her rounded abdomen. Dressed as she was in jeans and a T-shirt, with her long, blond hair flowing over her shoulders, he could have passed her on the street and never known she was one of country music's fastest rising stars.

"It's not nonsense, Mindy. You have to stop thinking like an amateur singer. The information these two will have could be worth a lot. We can't have them going around spilling information about you and Trey to the public."

"I think the physician-patient relationship covers that," Jared said as he headed up the stairs to meet their new patient, ignoring the irritating woman and her papers who had just insulted both him and Sky with her demands.

"I'm sorry," Mindy Carter said as she held out a slender hand to him and then to Sky, who had followed him up the stairs.

"Marjorie means well. It's just that all this," the young woman said, holding out her arms, "came at us really fast and we haven't been able to catch our breath in the last few months. She takes her responsibility as our agent very seriously."

"It's very serious business," the woman said when she caught up with them, her breath labored as she climbed the last step. "You can't trust everybody here like you could at home.

And the reality show is just making the media more gossip hungry."

"Aunt Marj, it's okay. The Legacy Clinic has a great reputation," a man Jared recognized as Trey Carter said as he stepped outside to join them.

"That's right, Miss Marjorie, and the two of us are thrilled to have this opportunity to take care of your family." Sky stepped toward the woman and offered her hand, her smile showing none of the dread that Jared felt.

"Look at us keeping the two of you standing out here. Please come in and I'll get you both something to drink," Mindy said. "We appreciate you coming here to talk to us. I know most doctors don't make house calls anymore."

"How about I get us all some iced tea and you sit down and rest?" Trey suggested, holding the door open for them to enter.

Jared stepped into the foyer, following Sky, and was surprised to see that it opened straight into a sitting area surrounding a massive stone fireplace. Across the room there was a table that could fit twenty easily, but still the room seemed comfortable enough with no sign of the glitz and glamour he had been expecting.

"You are not allowed to mention anything about Mindy and Trey's home to anyone until after the latest reality taping is aired tomorrow night," Marjorie said as she followed them into the sitting area and took a seat, not waiting for them to sit before raising those insulting forms at them again. "These aren't just to cover Mindy and Trey. The producer of *Carters' Way* is insisting on them too."

"Oh, we understand perfectly your concerns," Sky said, her voice dripping with a sweetness he hadn't known she possessed. "We'll be happy to take them with us and have the practice's legal team review them. But I think we can all agree that the most important thing we discuss today is Mindy and her baby. Don't you think?"

And as if Sky had performed a miracle, or an exorcism, the woman's eyes softened and she smiled for the first time. "Of course, nothing is as important as Mindy and the baby."

The doorbell rang and the woman immediately sprang into action, flying off her seat and heading to the door. "That should be the party planner."

"I know she's a bit much," Trey said as he set a tray with the tea glasses down on the short table beside one of the couches, "but she's just being protective. Once she gets to know you, she'll calm down. And if she likes you, she'll be just as protective toward you. She's really just a super animated teddy bear. Her bites are rare and her love is genuine."

Jared stared at the man, taken aback by words that could have described the grandmother he had just been thinking of earlier. "I understand. You're lucky to have her."

"So, Mindy, how have you been feeling?" Jared asked, changing the subject when Sky turned toward him, uncomfortable with the way she was studying him.

"I'm good," Mindy said, rubbing her hands over her abdomen.

"We received your records from your doctor and they show your due date as August 1, which would make you almost twenty-eight weeks. Does that sound right?" Sky asked.

"I'll be twenty-eight weeks this Thursday," Mindy said, moving to sit closer to Trey as he took the seat next to her.

For the next half hour they discussed everything from Mindy's medical history to her birth plan. When they came to her history of a miscarriage the year before, Jared saw Trey wrap his arm around his wife. It appeared that Trey's aunt wasn't the only one in the family that was protective. It was very evident that the relationship the couple shared wasn't just something they pretended for the cameras. They seemed to have the kind of bond that Jared never understood. In theory, yes, he understood the human need for companionship. But to trust someone with that much of yourself? To risk losing someone again? No, that was definitely not something he was capable of doing.

So why did looking at the two of them make him feel empty in a way he'd never felt before?

"They're a cute couple," Sky said, as he started the truck to head back to town. "I don't think we'll have any trouble working with them."

"I guess," he said.

"Didn't you like them?" she asked. She'd turned toward him. It always made him feel uncomfortable, being the focus of all her attention.

He'd watched her with Mindy while she'd done most of the questioning, which had really been an informal health review. She was naturally good with people. He wasn't sure if she interacted with other people like she normally did with him, though somehow he doubted it. It seemed he caught most of her unwanted attention whenever they were in a room together. She just couldn't help but try to get a rise out of him, as if there was some perverse part of her that liked to make him uncomfortable, though he didn't understand why.

But she hadn't been that way today. Today she'd acted professional, something he very much appreciated.

"It's not important that we like them. It's just important that we give Mindy and the baby the best of care, which is something I'm sure we will do."

"Thank you," Sky said, giving him one of those big smiles that always sent a spark of unwanted pleasure through him.

"What are you thanking me for?" He forced his eyes back to the road that led off the ranch, but not before he saw the lovely way her eyes mirrored her smile.

"For trusting me. For having faith in me. In us. I know you have a problem working with midwives."

His hands tightened on the steering wheel. He didn't want to relive the reason he had trust issues with midwives. Did Sky somehow know his history? Did she know that it had been a midwife that had delivered him? That while he'd taken his first breath his mother had been bleeding to death? He didn't want to expose that secret part of his life. It was his own private pain to endure. "I don't have a problem working with midwives. I just want to be available and prepared if I'm needed."

"Whatever," she said, shrugging her shoulders as if it didn't matter that he didn't want to discuss it with her. "What did you think about the request to interview us on the reality show? I think it would be a great chance to give Legacy House a plug if we can work it into the conversation. It could bring in donations from all across the country."

He was glad she'd changed the subject, though it was another one he didn't want to think about. He had to agree that it would be good to get more revenue coming into the home to lift some of the pressure from his father. And with everything his dad had done for him, it was a small thing to have to answer a few questions for the show.

"I don't understand why they call it a reality show. In what world is the Carters' life a reality? If they want a real reality show they need to have a show about an exhausted mom and dad who go to work every day for minimum wage so they can come home and sit around the table with their kids and worry about how they are going to pay the bills." At least, that was the reality that he'd seen when he was a kid in foster care. He hadn't been dreaming of a big house with huge fireplaces and horses running around in pastures. He'd just wanted to know there was someone out there who'd make sure he got his next meal.

"I guess people wouldn't find that entertaining enough. Though if they'd had a hidden camera at my grandma's house when me and my siblings had been growing up," Sky said, her voice filled with laughter, "we could have entertained the whole country with our antics at the dinner table. My grandma could have won an award just for all the ways she could cook the deer sausage my uncle Ben brought us. Not that we complained. We were just happy to get a meal."

"What about your parents? They wouldn't have wanted to be on your reality show?" he asked.

Sky's laughter died and Jared knew he'd asked the wrong question. But then, as suddenly as her laughter had stopped, it started again. "My parents couldn't take the reality of raising seven kids. If it hadn't been for my mom's mother we would have been homeless."

Jared sat up a little straighter. Was it really possible that he and Sky had come from such similar situations? Yet here she was laughing about her childhood while his memories before the Warners had adopted him were anything but humorous.

"How do you do that?" he asked, before he could stop himself.

"Do what?"

"You talk about your parents leaving you when you were a child, and it sounds like things weren't easy at your grandmother's house, but you just laugh it all off. How can you do that?" Maybe the question was a little personal, but he couldn't help himself. He had never understood Sky's happy-go-lucky life-style. For some reason, now that he'd learned more about her, it was suddenly very important that he did.

Sky didn't answer him for more than a few moments, and he wasn't sure that she was going to. He looked over to see her chewing on her bottom lip again, deep in thought. Then she took a deep breath and began. "I can't deny that at one time I was bitter about my childhood. I acted out as most teenagers do, I think, but now that I look back on it, I was mostly just angry. Living in a small town where everyone knew that we had been dumped by our parents wasn't easy on me or my siblings. Not that times had been easy before my parents left us.

"No one wants to feel that they were unwanted. But my grandmother was a special woman. When our parents left us, I was angry and scared. We didn't know her well. Our mom had only taken us to see her mom a couple times that I could remember. But from the moment we got there she acted like having us dumped on her was the best thing that had ever happened in her life."

Jared could definitely relate to that feeling. "So you just got over it?"

"I wouldn't say I got over it as much as I decided that I wasn't going to let their actions determine how I spent the rest of my life. Not that it was something that happened overnight. Life isn't that easy. Right when you feel like everything is going your way, there's always something, or someone, who decides you don't deserve to be happy."

Jared looked over to see Sky staring out the window. "Why do I feel like you are leaving something out?"

Sky turned and gave him a smile that was filled with more sadness than happiness. He'd never known that a smile could be so sad, and he didn't like seeing it on her face at all.

"I'm sorry. I didn't mean to make you uncomfortable."

His words sounded ridiculous even to himself. All his questions had been uncomfortable. He was asking her to share things with him that he didn't have the right to know. What had he been thinking? Was he so self-absorbed in trying to figure her out that he'd not considered her feelings? He certainly hadn't wanted to drag out all his own painful history for her to sort through.

"It's okay. And it isn't something I left out. It's someone." Sky sat up straighter beside him. He saw her chin had gone up and her eyes were staring straight ahead. She looked like someone preparing for a head-on battle. "I was engaged, or at least promised to be engaged, to my high school boyfriend. After graduation, he wanted to go off to college but all I could afford was community college. I thought everything was going great. I had gotten into the local nursing school and he was in pre-med. We had made plans for the future. Then, suddenly, he changed. The calls and messages just stopped. His first visit home, he brought a girl with him."

Jared glanced over at her. Her eyes had gone from hurt to hard and her lips were sealed so tight that he wasn't sure she'd ever smile again. "When I cornered him and asked him what was going on, he seemed shocked to think I had really expected him to abide by all the promises we had made to each other. Apparently, I wasn't good enough for the new life he'd planned. He didn't need a backwoods wife. He needed someone he could be proud of."

Jared's hands tightened again on the steering wheel. He'd had enough humiliating remarks aimed at him as a child to recognize the pain she felt. And he knew it didn't go away. You carried those scars with you for the rest of your life—though looking at Sky you would never know that she had been hurt that way. "You know that he was wrong, right? Any man would be proud of you."

"Maybe. But I know something even better now. I know it doesn't matter what a man thinks of me. What matters is that I'm proud of myself."

Jared's hands relaxed. He liked her observation better than his own.

"So yeah, that's my sad story. I've had some knocks in life, but haven't we all? I just choose to not let them hold me down. Life is short. I choose to enjoy it as much as possible and I think the key to that is having a positive attitude. And if some days I don't feel like smiling, I smile anyhow. There's a reason they say fake it till you make it. Besides, even though most people would think my life was hard, I wasn't alone. You're never alone when you have as many siblings as I do."

He spent the rest of the ride home listening to Sky tell stories of her and her family's escapades in the Tennessee mountains. She'd been more open and honest with him than he'd ever been with anyone. He'd never even confided about his life before the adoption to his own mother, the most caring woman he'd ever met. How was it that Sky could reveal such a painful thing about her past so easily?

Once they arrived back at the office, Jared was glad to get to work. Their house call to celebrity music stars had the office backed up with patients, so he grabbed a chart off his first examination room door and went to work.

It wasn't until later that night when he'd finally finished rounds and made it home that he let himself think about what Sky had told him about her family. For some reason he'd always assumed that Sky, with her over-the-top, happy-go-lucky nature, had come from one of those picture-perfect worlds. Somehow, finding that she'd survived the life she'd described that morning, while laughing through it all, gave him a new respect for her, though he wasn't sure about her statement about faking it. That didn't seem healthy to him. How long were you expected to fake it? Wasn't it better to deal with your feelings?

Not that he'd dealt with his own in a very healthy way. He didn't need a counselor to tell him that he let his past hold him back—his father had been telling him that for years. Yet now, hearing Sky's story, he found himself wanting to move past all those barriers he'd sealed himself behind.

But what then? What would happen if he let go of all the pain and loss he'd experienced as a child? What could his life be like if he chose to live like Sky? Jared had faced a lot in his life, but he knew that the possibility of letting go of the past and moving forward was the scariest thing he had ever considered doing.

CHAPTER FOUR

SKY STARED WITH more interest than was appropriate as one jean-clad leg followed the other one down the ladder from the Legacy House attic. She didn't need to see the brown head of hair that eventually followed the hard muscled body as he climbed farther down the stairs to know that they belonged to Jared. She'd seen his truck outside when she'd arrived. She'd known he was here. But knowing that Jared was here and then being treated to this version of Jared was not the same. This version of Jared looked nothing like he did in his white lab jacket, which was always neatly pressed and buttoned all the way up to its stiff collar. This Jared was much more interesting.

As he wiped his dust-covered hands against the sides of his jeans, she had the outrageous urge to reach out and brush those streaks of dirt off him. When he turned toward her, she clasped her hands behind her back just in case they decided to go rogue and get her into trouble.

"Good morning, Jared," she said, making sure her voice was filled with as much of her normal morning cheer as possible even while her heart rate was climbing up into the danger zone. She stared up into those deep brown eyes that were always so serious and couldn't help but wonder if she would ever know the real Jared. Even today, with his clothes covered in dirt, there was a tense line etched between his eyes as he studied her. After all she'd shared with him earlier in the week, she'd thought he'd be more relaxed around her.

"What are you doing here?" he asked.

"I brought some donated maternity clothes that I received from one of my patients. What about you? Looking for ghosts in the attic?"

He lifted an eyebrow. Yeah, it was a stupid question. Jared wasn't someone who would spend his time ghost hunting. It was more something that Sky herself might do. Well, maybe not ghost hunting, but she would enjoy going through any old trunks that might be stored in the attic.

"There's a problem with one of the electrical outlets in the living room. It looks like a squirrel or a rat might have gotten in and chewed on some wires. I'm going to get an electrician out here today to deal with it."

Okay, maybe searching through the attic wasn't a good idea.

A girl carrying a laundry basket came through the hallway and Sky moved to the side to let her get around them.

"Hey, Jasmine. How are you feeling?" Jared asked, the lines between his eyebrows coming together into a small knot now as he concentrated on the girl. Sky looked closer at the young woman who couldn't be more than eighteen. There were dark shadows below her brown eyes and her face had that puffy, swollen look that no midwife wanted to see. Her stomach was rounded and by its size she appeared to be in her third trimester.

The girl gave Sky a look that wasn't very trusting. "I'm Sky. I'm a midwife that works with Dr. Warner."

"I'm fine," Jasmine said, her voice flat. With her experience dealing with teenage patients, Sky knew that the word *fine* was used to give only the most limited amount of information. There was something off with Jasmine though. Her eyes weren't just tired, they were empty, something that Sky didn't normally see in healthy young girls who were expecting.

"Are you taking the blood pressure medicine I prescribed?" Jared asked.

"Yeah, Ms. Mason gives it to me every morning and checks my blood pressure twice a day just like you asked. But it makes me feel tired," Jasmine said, shuffling her feet and hitching the basket onto her hip.

"I'll talk to Maggie and see if she can bring you in to see me tomorrow. I might need to adjust your medications," Jared said, once again aware of how lucky they were to have someone as devoted to her job as house manager as Maggie Mason. "And we'll get another scan on the baby."

Jasmine's lips turned up in a half smile at the mention of the baby before she walked past them. She got to the end of the hall, then turned back toward them. "Thanks, Dr. Warner."

Sky waited till Jasmine had turned the corner and disappeared. "What's going on with her?"

Jared folded the ladder back up into the attic opening. "Physically, her blood pressure has been climbing for the last month. Mentally, I'm not sure. I can't get her to talk to me about it. I've asked her if she wants to talk to a counselor or if she would like another doctor, but she says no. It was one of the reasons I came by today. I want to check if Maggie has any idea what's going on with Jasmine."

The door to the attic slammed as Jared pushed it shut with more force than was necessary. This was the closest she had ever seen Jared to losing his temper. He really was worried about the girl.

"How about I talk to her?" Sky asked.

Jared looked down at her, his body close to hers in the small hallway. For a moment she forgot what they'd been talking about. Those rogue hands of hers wanted to reach out and walk down all those hard muscles clearly outlined by his shirt. It was a normal reaction by a woman attracted to a man, this need to touch that she was experiencing. With another man she might have expressed her interest.

But this was Jared. The only games she was allowed to play with him had to be silent and mostly platonic since they'd always been in the workplace. And most of the time he didn't even seem to enjoy those.

So why was she standing there ogling the man? It had to be this new relationship outside of the clinic that was causing all this confusion inside her. Yes, she'd admit, at least to herself, that she was attracted to Jared.

And though she had always told herself that

she just liked to tease him, there was a part of her that wanted him to notice her. To look at her, the woman, not the midwife. She'd been thinking about him ever since they'd visited the Carters. She'd told him almost all of her life story, something that had probably surprised her more than him. She didn't share her past with many people. She'd been judged for being abandoned and coming from almost nothing for most of her life, so now she refused to have people look at her with pity or judgment.

But Jared had done neither of those things. He'd even taken up for her, letting her know that her ex, Daniel, had been wrong, and expressing his belief that she was someone to be proud of.

She realized that she'd been staring at him for too long when his head tilted to the side, studying her deeply. "I mean... I'd like to help her and she might talk to me since I'm not involved with her care. How old is she? She looks so young. Well, everything but her eyes looked young. Her eyes are sad. Empty."

"She's seventeen. You see it too?" Jared asked, as if surprised that she could see that the girl was hurting.

"Yeah. Something is bothering her. She's due in what, three months?"

"She's almost thirty-two weeks. The baby has some intrauterine growth restriction. Another reason I'm worried about her," Jared said.

"I'm going to help Maggie today with some of the heavy cleaning. I'll try to talk to Jasmine. It's a lot to be pregnant and seventeen. I assume that she doesn't have a lot of support from her parents if she's living here." Sky tried not to judge Jasmine's parents. She remembered when her own sister had become pregnant at seventeen. It had been Sky that had been the most upset with Jill. The last thing Sky had wanted for her sister was to be in a situation where she was responsible for a child she was unable to care for. But their grandmother, even after spending the last ten years of her life raising them, had supported Sky's sister.

"Her mother came to the first few appointments with her. They seemed close. But then Jasmine asked me about moving into Legacy House. She's never told me what happened. And I haven't asked Maggie if she knew. I didn't want to make Jasmine feel like she couldn't trust her."

Sky was surprised by just how intuitive Jared was being. He'd always appeared so disconnected. Not uncaring—she'd seen him worry over his patients just like the rest of them did—he just didn't let very many people into his life. Or at least that was how it seemed to her. It could be he had a legion of girlfriends he left every morning when he headed to work.

Okay, that was ridiculous and it might have come from a bit of jealousy that she would prefer to ignore. Besides, whether or not he had women in his life wasn't the point. It was the fact that he seemed to hold himself back from being involved with the people he saw every day. People like her.

Maybe he just didn't find regular people interesting. Maybe that was why he tended to keep to himself. Or maybe he was actually studying them all. Maybe that was why he'd questioned her about her attitude toward her life.

She shook her head and tried to concentrate on the issues Jasmine might be having. That was what was important now. Not Sky's own insecurities. "I'll see what I can find out. And if there's some way for me to help her, I will. She might just need some reassurance that Legacy House will be here for her. If it's an issue with her parents… Well, I might not be the person to talk to but I'll find someone to help her.

If nothing else, I can be a friend to her. Someone she can reach out to if she needs someone."

"Right now the most important thing is to keep her blood pressure under control. If the medication doesn't help I'm going to put her on bed rest."

They started down the hall to the kitchen, where Sky knew she would find Maggie and some of the other staff preparing lunch. They'd been lucky to find someone like Maggie to run the home after the original manager, Mrs. Hudson, had retired. Maggie had spent most of her nursing career working in the office with the elder Dr. Warner. The fact that Maggie was her best friend Lori's mom made it even better.

Sky's phone pinged with a message and she pulled it from her pocket. She read the message twice, making sure she understood what Mindy was asking before she let out a squeal. "You are not going to believe this," she said to Jared, her hand coming out and grabbing his arm to stop him. "Mindy and Trey want us to come to the party they are having tomorrow night. The one Marjorie said all the country music stars were coming to."

She looked at Jared and saw none of the excitement she was feeling. "You have to come. The invitation is for the two of us. Together."

Still, he just stood there and looked at her. "Please?"

His shoulders slumped and she knew she'd won. She squealed again and threw her arms around his neck. His body tensed under hers, but she didn't care.

She, Sky Benton, from so far back in the hills of Tennessee that they had to pipe in sunshine, was going to an A-list party with all the music stars of Nashville. And she wasn't going to let Jared Warner ruin it.

CHAPTER FIVE

SKY WAS SPEECHLESS. After not being able to stop herself from talking nonstop on her first trip with Jared to Mindy and Trey's home, now she didn't know what to say. Her speechlessness surprised even her. She always knew what to say—or at least knew how to fake it. But this? This was too amazing. It was a dream come true for a little girl whose grandmother had listened to the *Grand Ole Opry* on the radio on Saturday nights.

The welcoming but overly large room she'd sat in just days earlier was filled with people. Some were people she'd seen on countless music award shows and others she recognized from the Carters' reality show. Some of the men were dressed in fancy suits while others wore jeans and cowboy hats. The women were dressed both casually and formally too.

And while Jared was dressed in an appropriate, if somewhat subdued, black suit, Sky had decided to go all out. With Lori's help, she'd found the perfect dress at a downtown boutique. Navy blue with a fitted bodice and a short flared skirt, the dress had enough glitter on it to make her feel glamorous and ready to party. It was a standout dress. One she had thought would give her the confidence she needed tonight.

Except now that she was here, seeing all of these beautiful, talented people, her confidence had disappeared as her memories of the past kept telling her that she didn't belong here. She did her best to shake them off.

"So, where do we start?" she asked Jared, glad to have him at her back. She'd been alone when she'd arrived in town after leaving her small hometown hospital. She'd never been to a city as big as Nashville before. But she hadn't run home then and she wasn't about to run home now. She'd decided that life was for living, not holding yourself back because you didn't believe you deserved something. This was a once-in-a-lifetime opportunity for her. She would not look back later with regret.

Before Jared could answer, she saw Mindy headed their way and Sky took a step toward her. After the first step, it seemed the next came easier. She could do this.

"I'm so glad you could come," Mindy said. Dressed in a flowing silver dress that accentuated her rounded abdomen, she was the most beautiful woman in the room.

"We're glad to be here," Sky said, taking hold of Jared's arm as that "I definitely don't belong here" feeling returned.

"Come in," Trey said as he joined his wife, wrapping his arm around her waist before holding out a hand to Jared. "Our producer was just asking about you. I promised to introduce the two of you."

"You're beginning to act like Marjorie. They just arrived. Can't they have a few minutes before you and Joe start talking business?" Mindy asked her husband.

"It's fine," Jared said. "I have some questions about the show and the interview they want to do that I wanted to talk to you about."

Mindy let out a heavy sigh, then linked her arm in Sky's. "Let me get you a drink and show you around. Don't get me wrong, I love Joe, but you'll get to meet him later. There are a lot more interesting people here that you need to meet."

Sky let go of Jared's arm and let Mindy pull her into the middle of the room. She looked back at Jared, who was already deep in conversation with Trey. She'd thought it would be Jared feeling out of place here, not her, but she'd been wrong. Of course, Jared had been raised in Nashville. Maybe that was why he wasn't showing signs of being starstruck like she was.

Just when she thought she'd gotten control of her nervousness about being around so many talented people, she was swallowed up into a crowd of the who's who of Nashville. There were singers and famous band members. There was even a Tennessee senator. Everywhere Sky looked, she saw another person she recognized from a video she'd enjoyed or a song she'd just been singing along with on the radio. By the time Mindy pulled her into the kitchen area, Sky was in celebrity overload.

"Would you like a drink?" Mindy asked her. "The bar is open in the family room, but I've got water and Cokes here."

"A water is fine," Sky said, taking a seat at the island, relieved to get away from the noise for a moment. "I'm sorry to pull you away from your guests."

"I need the break," Mindy said, taking the seat beside hers. "It's our first party to host in Nashville and I love it, but I don't think I was truly prepared for it."

"I can't imagine what the last year has been like for you. You have your first number one album. Your move to a new city. And then all the touring with the pregnancy. How do you do it all?"

"It's been wild, but it's the kind of crazy that we both love. And Trey has done everything he can to make it easier on me. Especially since the pregnancy. After the miscarriage he was very supportive, insisting that we decrease our tours for the next couple of months. But then everything took off. We had our first number one hit and we had to run with it. It was what we both had been working for and there wasn't a guarantee we'd get another chance."

Sky couldn't help but be a little envious of the relationship Mindy and Trey shared. What would it be like to have someone looking out for you? Someone who would be there when you got home? Someone you could count on? Someone you could share a dream with? But most importantly, someone you could trust not to break your heart? Sky had trusted her heart to someone before and she wasn't sure if she would ever have the courage to do that again.

Not that she had any right to complain. She dated often enough. She just made sure the other person always knew that she was only looking to have fun.

"We'd planned to wait a while before getting pregnant again after the miscarriage," Mindy said, rubbing her abdomen, "but this little one was meant to be. They're our special rainbow baby. The best surprise we could ever have hoped for. That's why we don't want to know the sex of the baby. We feel it should be a surprise until they're here."

Sky believed that all babies were special, but there was something so bittersweet about the babies that followed the loss of another child. "I love that. And you can trust that neither Jared nor I will share that information."

"I know. Jenny told me what a great experience she had with you as her midwife, but I was still nervous about meeting you."

"Why?" Sky asked. It had been only natural for her to be nervous about meeting someone like Mindy and Trey. They were stars. But her? She was just a simple midwife from nowhere Tennessee.

Mindy sighed and leaned back in her chair. "I knew that things were going to change if we ever made it to the top of the charts. And then there was the reality show. We'd just started to have a small amount of success when we agreed to the show. We were prepared to lose some of our privacy, but I wasn't prepared for the way the people around us changed."

Sky remembered how her friends and even some of her family acted when she'd made the decision to leave her hometown and head to the big city. She'd never understood why they couldn't see that there was nothing for her there. She'd been made to feel like she was letting them down even though they knew how hard it was to watch her ex walk around with the woman whom he'd decided fit his needs for a wife better than her.

"When a friend of mine let it out that I was pregnant, the media went crazy. We were so happy about the pregnancy, but we didn't want to share it yet. We'd just got over the media attention that my miscarriage received, and I'd made it plain to everyone who we told that I didn't want to share the pregnancy. Not yet, at least. We knew it would have to come out with the reality show and everything, but we wanted to wait. I guess I just didn't feel I could trust someone after that. But when I met you and Jared, you made me feel better. You were interested in me, Mindy, not Mindy Carter of the Carters. Does that make sense?"

"It makes perfect sense, and I'm sorry someone you thought you could trust let you down that way. I hope you know now that you can trust me. My goal is always to put mother and baby first. That's why I have a frank talk with all my patients as far as their birth plan. Your health and that of the baby will come first for me and Jared. Where they come from, their background, that's not a priority." Sky stopped to take a sip of her water.

"About Jared," Mindy said, "I hope it doesn't bother you that we asked to have the two of you work together. I really want a midwife to care for me, but Trey wanted to go the traditional route."

"It doesn't bother me. Jared and I are both happy to work with the two of you," Sky said. This was pretty much what Jack had told her and Jared the day he'd first spoken to them about Mindy and Trey. While Sky knew that some midwives would have been insulted by the request, she hadn't been. She knew that she could provide the care that Mindy and her baby would need. She'd reviewed Mindy's records closely and there were no risk factors that would keep Mindy from having a midwifery delivery. But if Trey needed the reassurance of Jared being involved, that was okay too.

"About you and Jared," Mindy said, her eyes

lighting up with humor, "am I imagining that there's something there besides work going on between the two of you?"

For the second time that night, she was speechless. She took a big gulp of water, paying close attention to swallow it without choking, then set the bottle down. She liked Mindy but she didn't know her well enough to admit her secret attraction to Jared. She wouldn't even admit that to Lori. "We're colleagues. That's all."

It was the truth, yet she felt a small amount of guilt for not admitting to her unexpected interest in Jared. Mindy had been open with her about her fears and how someone had let her down. It had been more than just the normal patient-and-provider sharing of information. This had been more personal.

There was something about Mindy that put Sky at ease. And it had helped put all the absurdity of the crowd in the other rooms into perspective for her. Not too long ago, Mindy was just a normal person working to make her dream come true, just like Sky had been when she'd worked to become a midwife. How many of the people out there surrounded now by fame and fortune had started just like the two of them? Like Jared had said, they put their cowboy boots on just like she did.

"Thank you for helping me get over my nervousness tonight." Sky set her bottle down again and turned to Mindy. "I'm not usually like this. It's just…my world is so much different than this. This is…"

"Extreme?" Mindy asked, standing and taking Sky's arm again.

"Yes!" Sky said as they headed back into the crowd, this time feeling more confident. "So, let's go get crazy too."

Jared looked over the crowd, trying to find Sky. He'd had a good talk with the producer of the Carters' reality show. While Sky didn't seem to have any problem being on the show, he didn't like the idea of opening up his personal life to the public. He knew it wasn't like he or Sky were going to be featured except for the small part of being health care providers for Mindy. Still, he'd made the producer promise that there would be no unnecessary information given out about the two of them. With the handsome donation the producer had agreed to for Legacy House, Jared knew he'd made the best of the situation that he could. They'd do an interview or two and it would be over with. Now he just needed to find Sky so they could leave.

Sometime since he'd left the party to join the producer Joe and Trey in his office, a band had set up. The music was good, of course—he wouldn't expect anything less with the caliber of musicians in the room. When a man he recognized as a Hall of Fame singer joined in with his own guitar, Jared stopped to listen for a moment. His own hands itched to feel those guitar strings under his fingers. To feel the vibration of the music flow into him along with the emotions it brought him.

When the song ended and the applause started, he made his way back through the crowd to the other side of the room, where a dance floor had been set up. The band started back with a line dance favorite from the 1990s and it only took him a minute to spot Sky among the dancers. Then he recognized the man she was smiling at beside her. Nick Thomas was a local boy who'd formed one of the top bands in the city. He hadn't gained the fame that most of the people in the room had, but from the local media reviews it was only time before his band hit it big.

But it wasn't Nick that held Jared's attention. It was Sky. And it wasn't the way her short skirt twirled around her shapely legs as she danced or the way her head of blond curls bounced with her movements. It was her smile. That happy, wide-mouthed smile that made him want to join her in the dance. That made him want to pull her to him and swing her around and around with the rhythm of the music until they both were breathless.

The song ended and she said something to Nick, then turned toward him. He knew the moment she saw him as their eyes locked and her smile changed to that mischievous one she loved to tempt him with. His body tensed with an edginess he'd never felt before as she walked slowly toward him. The crowd faded away as she took his hand and began pulling him toward the dance floor. The band started to play a slow, sad song filled with the sweet strains of a fiddle.

"Dance with me," Sky said, her blue eyes sparkling with a fevered excitement that flowed over onto him.

He knew he shouldn't. This wasn't a date. They were there purely as professional colleagues. Nothing more.

But as her arms wrapped around his neck, his own arms found their way around her waist, pulling her closer. And when she laid her head against him, he let himself relax against her. What could it hurt to share one dance?

It only took a minute for his body to answer that question. It was as if a fire had been lit inside him as his body reacted to the feel of Sky against him. His muscles tightened and he went stone hard. He tried to keep his breathing as even as possible as they swayed to the music, her body rubbing against him with each movement. He glanced down and their eyes met. As she drew in a breath that appeared as labored as his, his eyes went to her lips, the same lips that had teased him for months. For a moment he considered tasting them. Would they be soft and supple? Or would they be firm and needy? He had just started to lean down when the couple next to them bumped into him, breaking whatever spell he'd been under.

What could one dance hurt? It could destroy his whole reputation if he let himself lose control on the dance floor.

With a willpower he hadn't known he possessed, he pulled himself back from the brink of doing something that would scandalize the whole room. But when the song ended and she stepped away from him, his arms felt empty. It had only been one dance. The fact that her body had molded so perfectly to his didn't mean a thing. But he'd danced with many women before Sky and he'd never felt anything like this before.

"We should go," he said, though his traitorous feet refused to move.

"Why? Do we have plans?" she asked, her voice soft and breathy. His body responded as once more she stepped toward him.

He wanted to pull her back into his arms, to kiss that mouth that had teased him for the last six months. Only he couldn't kiss her now any more than he could have kissed her all those other times. He had to restrain himself just like he'd done over and over when she had tempted him. He needed to put things back to the way they'd been before that dance. Before he'd felt how right her body felt against his.

It should be simple. One step. Just take one step and walk away. But this was Sky. Nothing about the woman was simple. They constantly butted heads at work. She'd teased and tortured him for months with her sexy smile and sassy winks.

Someone tapped him on the shoulder and broke the spell that had held him captive. Turning, he saw that it was Nick standing behind him.

"If you aren't going to dance with the lady, I'd like to," Nick said, his oh-so perfect smile making Jared's teeth clench on the words he wanted to say.

"No. We were just leaving," Jared said, managing to get the words out before taking Sky's hand and pulling her behind him.

It wasn't until they were at the door that he was reminded of where they were and why they'd come. None of this was supposed to be about him and Sky. Nor was the possessive way he'd just acted professional.

It sobered him to know how close he'd come to making a scene by telling Nick right where to shove his invitation. They were there to represent his father's practice and to help gain more donations for Legacy House. He remembered how beaten down his dad had looked when he'd shared that Legacy House could be in trouble financially. And Jared had almost blown everything, nearly embarrassed his dad in front of the very people whose help they needed. His father deserved a better son than that.

He let go of Sky's hand and took a physical step away as his brain took a figurative step back from the line his body had been prepared to cross.

"I'm sorry," he said. "I shouldn't have spoken for you. If you want to go back to Nick I understand."

* * *

Emotions bounced around inside of Sky like she was a pinball machine. Shock with a small amount of pleasure from the way Jared had reacted to Nick's interest in her. Anger at the way he'd spoken for her without giving her a chance to tell the other man she wasn't interested. And finally, the worst part, pain from the way he was now prepared to let her return to Nick after the intimate dance the two of them had just shared.

She looked across the room to see that Mindy was involved in a conversation with one of last year's CMA winners. It felt rude to leave without thanking her for the invitation.

She looked over at the ramrod-straight statue that Jared had become and her anger pushed all of the other emotions out of its way. Stomping her high heeled feet through the crowd, she left Jared behind. She didn't care if he followed her or not.

She'd made it outside the house and halfway across the drive by the time Jared caught up with her. When he walked around to her side of the truck to open her door, she was already opening it. Changing her mind, she slammed it shut and turned on him.

"I don't understand you," she said, the truth

of the statement hitting her hard. She didn't understand him because he had never let her get close enough. She'd been teasing this man for over six months now, trying to get a response out of him. Yes, she wanted to make him smile, but now she wondered if it had been more than that. The more time they spent together, the more she wondered if she'd been secretly wanting him to seek her out. To return her interest.

And for a few moments tonight, she'd thought he had been interested. Then the old Jared who she'd watched turn away from her over and over found that control he was famous for, leaving Sky now confused and hurt. Why couldn't the man just relax and enjoy the moment? Had he not felt that all-consuming need for her that she had felt for him? Had she been the only one who had experienced that magical moment on the dance floor?

"I was having so much fun." She wouldn't cry, not in front of him. She'd promised herself that she would never cry again when someone walked away from her, yet the tears felt so close now. "And then you ruined it. Why? Why couldn't you have just enjoyed the moment? Was it me? Was it something I did?"

"We didn't come here to dance," Jared said,

his eyes emotionless and his body rigid as he ignored her questions.

How could this be the same man who had held her just minutes before? How could this be the same man whose body had reacted so eagerly to hers? Did he think she hadn't noticed the way his body had hardened against hers? Hadn't he felt the way she'd melted against the heat of him?

"Well, maybe you didn't, but I did."

"We were supposed to represent the practice and try to get donations," he said, his stern jaw turning up in challenge.

"We were supposed to blend in with the crowd while representing the practice and earning some goodwill for Legacy House. That was what I was doing with Nick. He's a good friend of Mindy and Trey's. They'd told him about what the home does to help local women. He's from Nashville. He was interested in helping."

"It wasn't Legacy House he was interested in on the dance floor. That wasn't why he wanted to dance with you."

"He wasn't the person I was dancing with. I was dancing with *you*. So maybe you should explain to me why it was that you agreed to dance with me? It certainly wasn't because you wanted to *represent the practice.*" She filled the last three words with as much sarcasm as was possible.

They faced each other, both of them breathless from the emotions that swirled around them. Along with the anger, she felt a certain thrill running through her because she'd been able to make Jared show at least some sort of emotion for her. He might deny how he'd responded to her on that dance floor, but she knew better. He'd felt something for her when he'd held her. He'd wanted her. And she'd wanted him.

Unfortunately, it was just as plain to her that he wasn't going to admit it. That for a few minutes she'd made him drop that facade of detachment he wore. And if it truly wasn't something he wanted, it didn't matter. He wasn't the first man that hadn't wanted her. Her ex had made that plain when after years together he'd walked away from her without a second thought.

"I'm sorry if I embarrassed you and the practice," Sky said. "That wasn't my intention."

"You didn't embarrass me."

All the emotions that she had been feeling drained out of her as suddenly as they had come. She felt empty and so very tired. She opened the door and climbed into the truck. She turned away from Jared when he climbed in beside her and started the engine.

She'd assumed she'd leave the party tonight floating on air after meeting all the famous people of Nashville. Instead, she wanted to dig a hole and climb into it to escape this familiar feeling of being unwanted.

Had she really thought she could blend in with people like those she'd met tonight? Jared had made it plain that she was only there because of the practice. She'd just been the hired help, at least that was what he thought. It had been stupid of her to think it was anything more than that.

Just like it had been stupid for her to think that sharing her secrets with Jared might have made a difference in how he saw her.

"Look, I just think it would be better if we remember that we are here to do a job. This isn't about us and all this..." he said, turning toward her and waving a hand between the two of them.

"This?" she asked, copying his waving hand gesture. "You mean the two of us acting human?"

Jared's eyes met hers and she saw a vulnerability there that surprised her. "What are you afraid of? Is it disappointing your father? Or is it me?"

She didn't want to think that there was something about her that scared him off from becoming involved with her. She had been over-the-top flirty with him, and sometimes she did push too hard when there was something that she wanted, but she'd only wanted him to notice her. "I'm sorry if I've been too pushy. I just thought…"

What had she thought? That he would jump at the chance of spending time with her on the dance floor? That he'd welcome her into his arms? That he'd secretly been harboring a crush on her just like she'd been harboring one on him?

"I just thought we could have a good time while we were here," she murmured, turning her head away from him so he wouldn't see the tears that she couldn't explain.

"It's not you, Sky. I just don't think the two of us getting involved would be a good thing. I'm sure you'll agree that the two of us are just too different. Things would get complicated."

He looked over at her as he started his truck, then sat there as if waiting for her to agree with him. Not that she did. All she knew was that when she'd been in Jared's arms, it had felt right. Finally, when she didn't speak, he put the truck in gear and started down the drive.

CHAPTER SIX

JARED WAS HAVING a bad day. From the time his alarm had gone off, nothing had gone right. He'd even growled at Tanya this morning when she'd reminded him that he had a lunch meeting with his dad and Sky at noon, though the office manager had only been doing her job He tried to tell himself it was just because it was a Monday and even he didn't like the first day of the workweek. But he knew it was more than that. He'd been in a foul mood ever since Friday night when he'd dropped Sky off at her home.

He knew he owed her an apology. He'd overstepped his place and in the process he'd ruined the night for her. He'd known she was excited about meeting all the famous people that had been sure to attend the Carters' party. He'd even overheard Lori talking to Tanya about helping Sky pick out a dress for the event. She'd wanted something to make her blend in with all those famous people.

Not that it had worked. She would never blend in with any crowd. She was too beautiful, too spirited for that. It was what drew Jared to her while at the same time making him want to be as far away as possible. He knew danger when he saw it and Sky was the most dangerous woman he'd ever met. She was like an atomic bomb that could blow the life he'd worked so hard to make right out of the Tennessee mountains. That was why he'd felt the need to remind Sky that nothing could happen between the two of them. But if he really believed that, why had he spent the rest of his weekend thinking about the dance the two of them had shared?

"Hey, Dr. Warner, can I speak to you for a moment?"

Jared looked up from his desk to see Lori's mom standing outside his door. "Sure, Maggie, and call me Jared, please."

"I don't want to disturb you, but they just took Jasmine back to the examination room and I wanted to talk to you before you see her," Maggie said as she stepped into the office. "You asked me to let you know if there were any changes with her blood pressure or her behavior."

Jared pushed the laptop he had been using out of the way. "How is she doing?"

"Her blood pressure is about the same with the medications you've given her and she is taking them without any trouble. It's her behavior that has me worried. She just seems so detached from the rest of the women in the household. She spends most of her time sleeping or at least in her bed."

"She told me the medication for her blood pressure was making her tired, but I don't think that's all there is to this. She's made too much of a change since she first came to see me with her mother. I'm wondering if she's homesick. Have her parents visited her?" He didn't know a lot about Jasmine and her parents' relationship. They'd seemed to be close on that first visit. Jasmine's mother had asked all the appropriate questions as a caring parent of a pregnant teenager. But something had happened between them, something big, and whatever it was, it had affected Jasmine badly. Sky had followed through on her offer to talk to Jasmine, but she'd told Jared that the girl had seemed very low energy and had no luck in getting her to open up.

"Her mother calls her I know, but the conversations I've heard were very short. From what I can tell, there was some type of disagreement between the two of them before Jasmine came to Legacy House. And as far as the medication is concerned, I don't think we can blame it for all of the changes. She's showing too many signs of a new onset of depression. I can't say she's not looking out for the baby. She's doing everything we ask as far as that is concerned. She's just not taking care of herself. There were times last week when she'd go days without bathing or dressing properly."

Jared sighed, then rose. They couldn't have found anyone to manage the home as well as Maggie did. With her medical background and her caring nature, she was the perfect stand-in mom for the women there. "Thanks for letting me know. I'll talk to her and try to get her to agree to see a counselor. Whatever is going on with her psychologically, it's not a good combination with her hypertension."

Maggie thanked him before returning to the waiting room, and Jared headed into the exam room to see Jasmine. Knocking and then opening the door, he saw immediately why Maggie had been concerned. The young girl lay on the examination table, not even opening her eyes when he entered. The last couple months with Jasmine had been like watching a thriving flower slowly wilt in front of him. There had to be something he could do to help this girl.

Pulling out his phone, he sent a message to Sky asking her to meet him in the examination room. He needed a second opinion along with any help he could give her. He hadn't seen Sky come into the office but he knew she normally had patient exams scheduled on Mondays.

"Good morning, Jasmine," he said, taking a seat and opening the room's computer where the patient's weight and vital signs had been recorded. Her blood pressure hadn't increased but neither had it decreased. He hated to add a second blood pressure medication but it looked like he was going to have to do it.

There was a knock on the door before Sky entered. She'd pulled her hair back into a pony-tail today and he found himself missing those curls of hers that spiraled all around her face. When her eyes met his, they were all business. Yeah, she was still mad at him. It was some-thing they'd have to deal with but it would have to wait till later. Right now his priority was his patient.

"Jasmine, Sky is one of the midwives here. You met her the other day."

Jasmine opened her eyes for the first time, then sat up at the end of the exam table. He noted the dark circles around the girl's eyes, but it was the increased puffiness in her face that truly bothered him. What had started out as a concern for hypertension was now looking more and more like preeclampsia.

"Hi, Jasmine. We talked the other day when I was helping Ms. Maggie."

"I'm not stupid just because I got myself pregnant," Jasmine said, the first sign of life showing in her defiant eyes. "I thought you were my doctor. Why do I need a midwife?"

"Sky and I work together on some cases. And neither one of us thinks you're stupid. If I remember correctly, your mother said you had earned a scholarship for college next year. What are you planning on studying?" He had her talking to him now and he didn't want her to stop.

"I was going to do pre-law, but that's messed up now. Everything is messed up now." Jasmine's shoulders lowered along with her head, that small spark of defiance gone.

"My sister is a lawyer. She practices family law in our hometown. What type of practice are you planning on going into?" Sky asked, taking a seat in the chair beside Jasmine as the girl looked up at her.

There was pain and disappointment in the girl's eyes now. Was that what was bothering her? Did she think that because she was having a baby she couldn't go to college? Couldn't have a future? She definitely wasn't like most of the teenagers she dealt with that were more concerned about the here and now. Jasmine had planned a future that hadn't included raising a child.

"I told you. It's all messed up now. My parents… It's just messed up and I don't want to talk about it. Ms. Maggie said you wanted me to come in so that you could check my blood pressure and adjust my medication. That's why I'm here." And there was that spark of anger again. He didn't like the fact that making her angry could increase her already too high blood pressure. Still, at least he had an idea what the problem was now.

"I'm going to change your blood pressure medicine and I want to do some more tests," Jared said. "And I'd still like you to consider going to see a counselor."

"I don't need a counselor. I don't need anything except to have this baby," Jasmine said before falling back against the table.

"You still have a few weeks until it will be safe for the baby to be born. I'm going to step out and get someone to come in and draw some blood. If you're okay with it, Sky can do a fast exam of your heart and lungs for me and check you for swelling while I'm gone."

Jasmine sat back up and looked Sky over from head to toe. "You still haven't told me why she's here."

"Like I said, we work together sometimes. It's good to get a second opinion, don't you think? We're working together right now with a famous country star." Jared saw the interest in Jasmine's eyes before it disappeared. "I'll send someone right in to draw that lab work."

He left the room, hoping that with some privacy Jasmine might open up further to Sky. A few minutes later Sky appeared at his office doorway. "They're drawing Jasmine's labs now. I was going to let her go after that, but I wanted to check with you first."

"Did she say anything else to you?" Jared asked.

"I mainly talked to her about where my sister went to school and some of the courses she took. She seemed interested at first. Then she went back to the same line she used before. Everything is messed up because of the pregnancy. I don't know what happened between her and her parents, but I'm pretty sure that's at least part of the source of the depression she's having now. I'm supposed to help Maggie again Wednesday. I'll talk to her again then."

"At this point her blood pressure has got to be my main concern. And now that she's starting to have more swelling, I'm beginning to suspect she's becoming preeclamptic." Like the poor girl didn't have enough going wrong for her. "She could really use her parents' support right now, but I can't contact them without her okay. Maybe you can mention that?"

"I'll try to bring it up to her. She's seventeen. Whatever it is going on in that head of hers seems insurmountable right now. Hopefully, she'll let one of us help her." She started to turn away.

"We're supposed to have lunch with my father today," Jared said. He had to find a way to apologize for his actions Friday night but now didn't seem like the right time.

"Tanya reminded me. I'll meet you there." With that, Sky turned and hurried down the hall toward her own set of examination rooms. He probably owed her another apology for taking her away from her own patients. Not that she would be interested in one. She was just as worried as he was about Jasmine.

It seemed like the two of them would be working together even more now. And Jared found, even though he was well aware of the dangers after their dance, that he didn't mind that at all.

Jared and his father were waiting for Sky when she arrived at the Barbecue Shack down from the office. Unlike its name, the place was more modern barn chic than a shack. A large brisket turned in the rotisserie pit at the front entrance and the sweet smell of roasting meat pulled a nice crowd inside throughout the day.

She spotted both of the Warner men at a corner table, their heads together as they studied the menu. She still didn't understand why they couldn't have met in Jack's office, but when Tanya told you to be somewhere you just followed instructions.

"Sorry I'm running late," she said as she took a chair across from them. "I had a heavy load of patients this morning."

"I meant to thank you for helping me with Jasmine. I know you had your own patients to see," Jared said, his distant politeness setting her teeth on edge, though she shouldn't have been surprised by it. He'd made it clear that he didn't want anything to do with her except professionally.

"I didn't mind. I just don't know if I did any good. I'm going to talk to my sister tonight and see if she has any advice for someone with a child wanting to go to law school. I'm sure there are resources out there to help single moms like Jasmine." Sky kept her voice just as polite as his.

Dr. Warner followed their conversation, his head ping-ponging back and forth between them, without commenting. As always though, his eyes showed a merriment that Sky herself wasn't feeling.

"Again, thank you," Jared said. His words were sincere. They shouldn't have hurt.

"It's nice to see the two of you working together so well. I knew the two of you would find a way to make this work," Jack said as the waitress appeared to take their order.

After she left, Jack pulled out his phone and held it out to them. "I received this from our accountant this morning. It seems that you two and the Carters have been talking up Legacy House to a lot of people in their circle. We received four significant donations over the weekend. I don't know the last time we've received donations like this, so keep up the good work. You're making a difference in a lot of women's lives."

Sky skimmed down the email till she got to the names listed and the amounts that had been donated. She recognized two of the names, one being Nick and the other the producer of the Carters' reality show.

"Joe promised another twenty-five thousand for allowing him an interview for the show. Also, he is going to let us put a plug in for Legacy House in the interview."

"Why would they want to interview us? There's nothing exciting about the two of us." It would be good to get Legacy House on the show though. Maggie had been talking about needing to update some of the kitchen with large appliances. And she'd said that the electrician had recommended an electrical upgrade too.

"I think it's just to get more interest in the show. The audience seems to be obsessed with Mindy's pregnancy," Jared said, acting like it didn't bother him that people could be asking them personal questions when she knew it would be the last thing he wanted.

"And how are things going with Mindy and

Trey? It sounds like they are satisfied with their care so far," Jack said.

"Mindy's coming in Friday for her first visit. I'm going to let her in through the employee entrance so she won't have to come through the waiting room. I'm not expecting any problems as far as the pregnancy. She's done well so far. I do want to get an ultrasound to measure the baby's growth while she's there. What about you, Jared? Anything I'm forgetting?"

"It sounds fine. Except for her miscarriage she doesn't have any risk factors. Trey did specify that they didn't want to know the sex of the baby. It is really important to them to find out at the delivery."

"Well, that all sounds good," Jack said as their food arrived.

The rest of the meal they spent discussing what Jack wanted them to stress in the interview as far as the practice was concerned and Legacy House. It was like prepping for an examination and Sky wanted to make sure she was ready for any questions that might be directed at her.

She launched herself into her afternoon patients' exams feeling better than she had that morning when she'd come in. She and Jared had managed to share a lunch without either of them referring to the party they'd attended together. And if he wanted to pretend that the dance they had shared had never happened she could do that too. It had only been one dance, she told herself.

So why did it feel like it had changed everything?

CHAPTER SEVEN

WITH THE OFFICE closed and most of the staff gone for the day, Sky sat back in her chair and perched her bare feet on the desk. She'd gotten a blister on her foot while dancing Friday night and being on her feet all day had just aggravated it.

When the knock came on the door, she assumed that it was one of the techs saying goodnight. As Jared stuck his head into her office door, she started to put her legs down, then stopped. It was her office after all. If she wanted to put her feet up after hours, she could do it.

"Sorry, I don't mean to disturb you. I just wanted a minute of your time," he said. He was still being overly polite and she still didn't like it. He'd made it clear that he wasn't interested in her except professionally, But he didn't have to act so cold to her.

"Is there something we didn't cover at lunch concerning the Carters?"

"That's not what I wanted to talk about. I just wanted to tell you that I'm sorry for what happened. I know you were excited about the party and I'm sorry I ruined that for you."

Sky didn't know what to say. She *had* been excited about the party. And it had been amazing. She'd had a great time dancing with some of country music's biggest stars. She had enjoyed getting to know Mindy better too. But the thing she had enjoyed the most was the one thing Jared was apologizing for.

And why did they have to go over this again? Oh, he said he was sorry for ruining the party, but she knew what he meant. He was embarrassed that he had responded to her on the dance floor. The point being, *he had responded to her*. They both knew that. She just didn't understand why he was determined to ignore it. The two of them were single adults. And it wasn't like workplace relationships didn't take place there. As long as they were discreet, no one would care. There was something else keeping him tangled up that he couldn't seem to break free of. Something stronger than his desire to explore what the two of them had felt that night. If only she could understand what it was.

But that wasn't something she was going to

solve tonight. "I enjoyed the party. You didn't ruin it for me."

Her phone rang and she almost groaned when she saw it was the women's unit of the hospital. "This is Sky."

She listened as the nurse on the labor floor gave her report on one of her patients who was thirty-six weeks and expecting twins. Sky had been her midwife for her other two deliveries and they had hoped that she would be able to deliver both of them vaginally. Now it didn't look like that would happen.

"I'll be over to talk to her," she said before ending the call. "Are you on call tonight for surgery?" she asked him.

"I am. Why? What's wrong?"

"Nothing's wrong. I have a patient that is expecting twins. They were both head down on her ultrasound last week, but it looks like baby B decided he didn't want to follow his sister's direction. He's complete breech now." Sky put her feet down and toed her shoes back on. "Sarah's water is broken but she's only two centimeters and not having regular contractions yet. I delivered her other two babies without any difficulty, but she has a small outlet. We planned to try for a vaginal delivery with the twins if they were both cephalic, but I don't feel good about trying to turn baby B."

"I'll call over and tell them to get her ready for a C-section," Jared said. "Have you discussed with her the possibility of surgery with twins?"

"Of course I have. It was one of the first things we discussed. I know how to do my job, Jared." Why did he always make her feel like he thought she was incompetent? "When are you going to accept that midwives are as competent as doctors? What is it you have against us?"

"I know you are competent. I didn't mean anything by my question," Jared said. "I don't know this patient. I'm just asking for information."

"It isn't just this time. You said you don't have a problem with midwives, but you do it all the time. Is it something I've done?" She knew this wasn't the time to get into this, but she needed to know. She was tired of feeling like she wasn't good enough for him. Like she was lacking something. She knew that no matter how much she denied it, some of her insecurity came from the way her ex had treated her. Still, she wanted to know that Jared trusted her to take care of her patients. "What do I have to do to convince you that I'm a good midwife?"

The sincerity in Sky's blue eyes cut through his need to keep his most painful history private. "It's not you. It's just…"

He took the seat at the desk across from her. How was it that this woman had the power to make him bare his soul to her? "My mother died after childbirth."

"I'm so sorry, Jared," Sky said. "Do you want to tell me what happened?"

This was something that he didn't speak of to anyone, but he found himself now wanting to explain it all to her. Maybe then she'd understand that it wasn't that he doubted her capability. He just wanted to make sure what had happened to his mother didn't happen again.

"After I was born, my grandmother told the midwife taking care of my mother that something was wrong. My mother had begun complaining of feeling bad, feeling 'funny.' My grandmother had no medical training, but she told me she felt it in her soul that something was wrong. But before she could insist that the midwife do something my mother had a seizure. She aspirated and coded while the midwife was repairing her episiotomy. She had an anoxic brain injury and a week later she was declared brain dead and removed from life support. My grandmother discovered later that my mother's blood pressure had been rising during her pregnancy but the midwife hadn't followed up and ordered any of the diagnostic lab work she should have." He didn't tell her that his grandmother had blamed that midwife for the loss of her only child from that day until her death, while he'd grown up blaming himself. It had only been when he'd been older and had learned more about childbirth that he had understood the things his grandmother had told him.

"I'm so sorry that happened to your family," Sky said. "You didn't become a doctor because of Jack, did you? You became an obstetrician because of what happened to your mother."

"Jack was a part of it." He'd come to believe that having Jack, one of the most sought out obstetricians in Nashville, as his father had been more than fate. "But yes, most of it was because of my mother. I don't want another woman to die unnecessarily."

"That's what I want too. What we all want. But even with all the medical gains in our field, maternal deaths still happen," Sky said.

"That's why we have to work harder to find

ways to stop it from happening." Jared leaned forward, his hand reaching out to her in his need for her understanding. "Don't you see, Sky. That's why I double-check everything. I know I can be a bit intense, but I only want what's best for the patient."

"That's what we all want. Maybe working together, respecting the role each of us play in our patients' care is the best thing for our patients," Sky said, taking his hand and giving it a comforting squeeze. "Thank you for telling me about your mother."

Jared looked down to where their hands were joined. He felt as if a burden had been lifted from his shoulders. As if telling Sky had opened up something inside him. Maybe she was right? Maybe instead of working at cross-purposes, they could work together to ensure their patients' safety.

"Speaking of patients," Jared said as he let go of Sky's hand, "we need to go take care of those twins of yours."

"I'd like to assist you in surgery, if that's okay with you?" Sky asked as she stood and stretched. Jared knew that her day had been just as long as his.

"I think that would be a great idea," Jared said, rising and following her to the door.

"Okay, then. Let's go deliver these twins. I can't wait to meet the little troublemaker who decided he wanted to take his own path instead of following his sister." Sky took her jacket from the stand where she'd hung it.

"I think that sounds like a plan we can both agree on," Jared said, excited about the delivery. He told himself he was just looking forward to the birth of the twins, but he knew that having Sky right there beside him would make it even better.

"Hey, let me help with that," Sky said to Lori, grabbing one of the bags of groceries that her best friend was juggling as she tried to open the kitchen door to Legacy House.

"Thanks." Lori moved back so Sky could open the door. "Mom told me you would be here today. She appreciates all the help you've been with the spring cleaning. Though I don't know how you have the time with everything going on right now."

"I love helping out. I can't donate a lot of money so I give the time I have available instead."

"So how did the party go? I heard you and Jared got some significant donations," Lori said as they began putting away the groceries.

With everything going on in the office, Sky hadn't had a chance to tell her about that night. "It was amazing. It was like attending one of those parties you see pictures of after the CMA show. And Mindy was the perfect hostess."

"What about Jared? Did he have any fun?" Lori asked.

Sky grabbed a couple sodas from the fridge and sat them on the table. "I'm not sure. It's complicated."

"What do you mean?" Lori joined her at the table. "He didn't talk to you?"

It wasn't the talking that Sky was thinking about. She still couldn't get over how Jared had gone from hot to cold so fast. She hadn't planned to discuss any of what had happened between them with anyone, but maybe she needed to. Maybe talking with Lori would help her understand how he could change from one moment to the next. Or maybe it was her. Maybe she had just imagined the red-hot need that had flowed between the two of them.

"We talked. It wasn't the talking that was the problem. Well, at least it wasn't a problem until after the dance we shared."

"Really? What happened? Is he a bad dancer? Did he step on your feet?" Lori smiled, her eyes filled with amusement.

Was he a good dancer? She really couldn't remember much about the dancing or the music that was playing. She only remembered how perfect it felt to be in Jared's arms and how much she had wanted to stay there. And his eyes. She remembered the heat that had filled them. He'd wanted to kiss her, she was sure of that. "I think it was more like he stepped on my heart."

The amusement in Lori's eyes died. "Tell me what happened. Then give me a good reason I shouldn't kick his butt."

"You can't kick his butt. He's our boss's son. Besides, he didn't do anything wrong. At least, not intentionally."

"Tell me everything," Lori said.

So Sky told her. She told her about the people she met. How she had felt out of place amongst all the famous and talented people, though they'd all been kind and welcoming. She told her how Mindy had been especially sweet. Then she told her about dancing with Nick Thomas.

"What is he like? Is he going to call you?"

"I don't think he'll be calling me. Jared was pretty rude to him." She wondered if Jared would be calling Nick to apologize. She didn't think so.

"Jared? Our Jared? I've never heard him raise his voice before. It's like human emotions are something too menial for him."

"He's not like that, not really," she said, not liking the way Lori made him sound.

"Has anyone seen Ms. Maggie?" a voice asked from the doorway.

Sky turned to find Jasmine, still dressed in her pajamas. The circles under her eyes were even puffier than the last time she had seen her.

"I'll go get her," Lori murmured, giving the young girl a worried look.

"Come, sit down," Sky said. At first she thought the girl was going to refuse. But after glancing behind her, Jasmine took a seat across from her. "How are you feeling today?"

"I'm okay. Just still tired. Dr. Warner changed the medication but I'm still tired all the time. I'm getting behind in my classes."

That was the most Sky had heard the girl volunteer in any conversation. "I'm sorry. I'd be glad to help. Or Ms. Maggie knows several tutors that help with the students here. You're doing online courses, right?"

"I had to change when I got here. I was ahead of the class at my school." The words lacked the teenage sarcasm she'd been filled with earlier in the week. "And now I'm falling behind because of this stupid medicine."

"You're right. The medicine can make you feel bad. But I don't think that your being behind in your classes is all that is bothering you. Talk to me, Jasmine. Tell me what is wrong so I can help you."

"You can't help me. No one can now." Then the girl broke.

Sobs wracked Jasmine's body and Sky moved to put her arm around her. Over the girl's shoulders, she saw Maggie and Lori come into the room. Sky shook her head at them and they stepped back out.

"I can't promise to have the answer but I'm here to help if I can. You can't keep all of this bottled up inside of you. It's not good for you or the baby."

"It's the baby that's the problem," Jasmine said, looking up at her with eyes filled with tears she'd clearly been holding in for months. "I don't want to keep the baby. I know I'm being selfish. But I had my life planned. I've wanted to go to college for as long as I can remember."

"You can still go to college. You know that, right?" Sky didn't think that was the real problem but she wanted to make sure that Jasmine knew she had options.

"I know, but it won't be the same. I love this baby. I do." The girl's eyes begged Sky to believe her. "But I'm not ready to raise him. He needs someone that can do a better job than me. He deserves that."

Sky agreed with her that every baby deserved to be loved and cared for. If Jasmine didn't think it was something she could do, they needed to respect that.

"And there are a lot of people that would love him if that is what you want. Allowing someone to adopt your baby isn't something to be ashamed of. It's not selfish. It's one of the bravest things someone can do." Sky had been through that struggle before. "You know my sister, the one who's a lawyer?"

"You said she practices family law," Jasmine said as she wiped her eyes with the sleeve of her pajama top.

"She had a baby when she was just a little younger than you. She decided she wasn't ready to raise a child too. Her doctor put her in touch with an adoption agency and she found the perfect couple for her baby. They're very open about the adoption and my sister gets pictures and cards from them."

"My parents would never agree to that. They want me to keep the baby. They keep promising they'll help, but that isn't the problem. I'm just not ready to be someone's mom. I know that makes me a bad person."

"You're not a bad person. It takes a lot of courage to admit that you can't do something. And you're thinking about what is best for your baby." Sky hugged the young girl to her. Jasmine was being forced to make an adult decision about her baby when she was not much more than a child herself. She wanted to offer to speak to Jasmine's parents herself, but she knew it wouldn't help. Whether it was fair or not, Jasmine had to make that move herself.

"How about I get my sister to call you? She won't try to push you either way. It's a personal decision, not hers or your parents. She'll be honest with you about the process and how it has affected her life."

"That would be good. Did your parents try to talk her out of the adoption?"

"No. They weren't in our lives then. They left us with our grandmother when we were young. But my grandmother was ready to support her no matter what decision she made. Your parents might not agree with you, but I have the feeling that they will support your decision once you explain how you feel. They love you and want you to be happy. Just talk to them. Be honest with them."

Jasmine sighed and had just begun to stand when Maggie and Lori came back into the room. Sky had figured they were outside the door listening.

Maggie started fixing lunch. Jasmine volunteered to help, then Sky and Lori got up to join them. The girl still looked worn to the bone. It would take more than a talk with Sky to help her get back on track, however moving around and working instead of staying in bed and worrying was a first step.

CHAPTER EIGHT

SKY OPENED THE back office door and let Mindy inside. Dressed in a plain black hoodie that covered her hair, the country music star had none of the glamour that she was known for. In a worn pair of jeans and a pair of sneakers, she could have been any other patient in the practice. As Sky led her down the hall to her exam room, members of the staff walked by them without anyone looking twice.

She shut the door as Mindy pulled off the hoodie. "That's a pretty good disguise."

"Trey agreed to let me come by myself if I wore one of his old sweatshirts," Mindy said. "It actually was kind of fun sneaking in the back. Not that I want my life to always be like this."

Sky had a feeling Mindy hadn't accepted all the changes stardom was going to make for the rest of her life.

"Speaking of sneaking around, I didn't see you leave the party," Mindy said.

"I'm so sorry I didn't tell you we were leaving. It was kind of sudden."

"That wasn't a complaint. After watching you and Jared on the dance floor, I understand why you'd want to leave so fast. Though I'm confused about why you told me there wasn't anything happening between the two of you. That dance made it pretty plain that there's something between you."

"There wasn't. I mean, there *isn't* anything. We're just colleagues." Sky felt the flush of embarrassment flood her face. Now she definitely would look like she was lying. "Seriously, Mindy, we aren't dating."

"Honey, I know what I saw. The two of you were into each other. Even Trey said something about it after you left." Mindy's smile turned mischievous. "Though apparently Nick Thomas had his head in a barrel—either that or he needs glasses. He asked me for your phone number after you left."

Sky didn't know what to say to that bit of news. "We talked about Legacy House. He probably just wants some more information."

Nick seemed like a nice enough guy. There just hadn't been that connection she felt with

Jared. That attraction that drew her to him whenever he entered the room. Of course, that same attraction made him push her away every time they got close.

"I'm going to let Jared know you're here, then I want to get your vital signs and measurements," Sky said as she pulled out her phone to text Jared. "Have you had any new issues this week? Any cramping? Swelling?"

She was hoping to change the subject from her and Jared quickly. The last thing she wanted was for Mindy to say something in front of him.

"No. I feel perfectly healthy. I just wish Trey wasn't such a worrier. By the time I have this baby he'll have me swaddled in bubble wrap," Mindy complained as Sky helped her up onto the examination table.

Glad that Mindy was willing to let the subject go, Sky went through the exam quickly. When Jared knocked on the door, she already had Mindy draped and the ultrasound machine positioned.

"Okay, let's see how this little one is growing," Jared said as he moved the ultrasound wand over Mindy's abdomen. Within minutes he had all the measurements. And when the baby decided to give them that perfect view that would let them know its sex, Sky quickly changed the screen's direction.

"Everything looks perfect. The baby measures right at thirty weeks, which almost perfectly matches your due date," Jared said. "Would you like me to get a picture to send home for Trey?"

"I'd love that. He had planned to come, but there was some problem with the production of this week's show that he wanted to clear up. He and Joe get along well, don't get me wrong, but Trey knows Joe's job is to hype up the show with as much drama as possible. Sometimes he has to reel him in."

Jared handed Mindy a towel so she could wipe off all the ultrasound goo. "Joe's coming in Monday to interview the two of us here in the office after hours."

Sky looked over at him. She'd known that the interview was coming up. But Monday? She just hoped that Joe wouldn't ask any personal questions. The show was named *Carters' Way*, so she assumed they'd just be asked a couple questions in general about the care they gave their patients and maybe a question concerning the way the two of them were working together.

She was still thinking about the interview as she walked Mindy to the office's back entrance.

"I feel I should give you a heads-up about the interview," Mindy said as she adjusted the hood over her head. "Trey and I weren't the only ones who saw what was happening between you and Jared at the party. Trey was with Marjorie when you were dancing together."

"It was just a dance," Sky said as she opened the back door for her.

"You better keep practicing that line. Maybe Marjorie will believe it." Mindy grinned, then sprinted out the door toward her car.

As Sky stood and watched the country star get in her car, she repeated the words over and over, practicing putting emphasis on different words. "It *was* just a dance. It was *just* a dance. It was just a *dance*."

By the time she'd gotten back to her office, she had even almost convinced herself.

When Jared had agreed to a one-on-one interview, this wasn't what he was expecting. He'd assumed that the producer had meant to interview them himself. Instead it was Marjorie, wearing another red suit, sitting across from them. Her first couple of questions concerning their education and qualifications he had been prepared for. They each talked about the colleges they'd attended and where they had done residency. Sky managed to get in a few comments about Legacy House and the work they did there, but then something about Marjorie changed. There was a gleam in her eyes that put him on guard. This must be what a poor mouse felt like right before a snake went in for the killing strike.

"I can't tell you how happy Mindy and Trey are to have you and Sky taking care of Mindy and the baby. They've made several comments about how well the two of you get along." Marjorie's eyes took on a predatory look as her hands with their metallic red finger nails clasped together and she leaned in toward him. "And after seeing the way you were together at the party, I can see why. The two of you on a dance floor can really heat up a room."

He was stunned. This wasn't the type of question he had been expecting.

"Jared does look good on a dance floor, doesn't he? And we did enjoy the party." Sky's smile was perfect and there was sincerity in every word she said. "I can't thank Mindy and Trey enough for inviting us."

For a moment he thought Sky had shut down Marjorie on the subject of the party. Then the woman turned back to him and he suddenly felt like the weakest link.

"Jared, what about you? Sky seems to think you look good on the dance floor. How about her? What was it like to dance with this beautiful woman? It was plain to see that she was the hit of the party. Nick Thomas sure seemed to think so."

Why did the mention of that man's name bother him so much? It was time to get this interview back on track. "Sky is a beautiful woman inside and out. Her patients love her."

"I'm sure they do." Marjorie's eyes bounced between the two of them.

She was looking for another angle to go at him. He had to cut her off. "I just want to assure the audience that Mindy is in the best of hands with Sky. Working together, I know that we will be able to give the Carter family the best care in the country."

"I'm sure you will," Marjorie said, her eyes narrowing in warning that she'd come after them if they didn't take care of Mindy and her baby. Then she smiled. "You know, right now the two of you are almost the only people who know the sex of Mindy and Trey's baby. It seems that all of Nashville is wondering whether it will be a girl or a boy. Someone has even started an online betting pool. How does it feel to have such exclusive information?"

The woman seemed determined to find some kind of drama for this interview. "Actually, it's something we are very familiar with handling. Some of our patients want to wait till their baby is born to discover the sex."

"But I have to tell you, Marjorie, it *is* exciting having a secret that big," Sky said. Then leaning in to Marjorie, she whispered just loud enough for the camera to hear her, "But I'm still not telling."

The cameraman stopped filming. Marjorie clapped her hands together. "That was perfect, Sky. The sponsors will love it."

Jared had no idea why Marjorie was so excited, but if it kept her away from trying to hype up some type of romantic connection between him and Sky he was glad to go along with it.

As soon as he'd shown Marjorie and her cameraman out the door, he hunted down Sky in her office.

"Please explain to me what just happened," Jared muttered.

Sky gave him a smile then slung a bag over her shoulder as she headed for the door. "Marjorie wasn't going to let us go without getting something more exciting than the name of what colleges we attended. I watched this season's opener this weekend. It's a nice enough show, but there isn't a lot of drama because they are basically a happy couple. Happy couples don't draw ratings. I could tell that Marjorie and Joe wanted us to hype up the pregnancy. I just added a dramatic flair to the truth. We might know the sex of Mindy and Trey's baby, but we aren't going to tell anyone."

"So the questions about the party weren't just because Marjorie was being nosy? She was looking for some dirt to spread around?" Sky nodded, but it still didn't make sense to him. No one cared about two unimportant health care providers. It wasn't a glamorous job like being a country music star.

Which reminded him of Nick. "And I guess she was just trying to tie you and Nick together for ratings too?"

"Maybe," she said as he followed her down the hallway.

"I'll have to tell him about it the next time I talk to him." Sky opened the back door and when she turned to face him, he recognized that impish smile of hers.

Then after a wink that made his heart skip

a beat, she walked away, leaving him wanting to follow her. And not for the first time that week, he regretted that he couldn't do just that.

CHAPTER NINE

SKY HAD PLANNED a nice quiet Saturday. Instead she found herself sitting next to Jared on the Carters' band bus on the way to a concert in Knoxville.

"You didn't have to come," Sky said, before she spun herself around in the swivel chair set up at one of the tables in the bus.

"You're going to make yourself sick if you keep doing that," Jared pointed out. "And I did have to come. We're in this together. Remember?"

When Sky had received the phone call from Mindy asking if she could tag along for the tour stop, she'd been too excited to go to ask many questions. But after seeing Jared there and finding out that Trey's worry had caused Mindy to call Sky because she hadn't been feeling good, the trip had changed from fun to one of professional concern. Still, if you had to work on a Saturday night, you might as well enjoy yourself. And with a bus designed for comfort, this wasn't a bad trip.

"Of course, I remember," Sky answered. "But Mindy is fine now. I checked her blood pressure and she denied having any contractions. You could have stayed at home."

Not that she really minded him being there. He'd dressed the part tonight in jeans and a chambray buttoned-up shirt. His black boots had been shined to perfection. If she gave him a cowboy hat, he would have looked like another member of the band. With her own short, denim skirt and her brown, knee high boots, they both looked like part of the band, which worked out well since Mindy was adamant that no one suspect there were any worries about her health.

A couple of the band members came out of a back area, carrying their instruments. In minutes they were playing one of their new hits that had just come out. Sky smiled and tapped her bootheel to the rhythm. This was so much better than sitting around her house and doing her laundry.

She looked over at Jared and was surprised to see that he was enjoying the music just as much as she had. When she smiled at him and he smiled back at her, she thought her chest would burst open. Was this the real Jared? The one she'd caught a glimpse of while dancing with him, the one who'd opened up to her about his birth mom? She'd always known that he was holding back something. Hiding some part of him away from everyone. Was he so afraid of letting someone in that he hid that smile, those emotions of happiness and the joy of living, from everyone?

Then to her surprise, he picked up a guitar that had been lying on the table and began to play along with the band members.

Sky didn't move, afraid she'd break the spell that the music had wrapped around Jared. She listened with awe as the band changed the song, flowing into another one, an older song about loss and pain. It was a drinking song that had been redone by many music stars and it only took a few seconds for Jared to catch up with the rest of the group. They played for half an hour before the musicians set down their instruments and, after shaking Jared's hand and inviting him to play with them again, they disappeared into the back of the bus to change for the concert.

"That was amazing," she said when they were once more alone. "Why didn't I know that you could play?"

"I have my secrets," He said. His face was flushed with color. Embarrassment? He'd always had a confidence that Sky had admired, but she'd really only spent time with him at work until the last two weeks.

"Tell me one?" She loved seeing this side of him. Maybe if she kept him talking he wouldn't notice how much of himself he was allowing her to see.

"Like what?" he asked, his hands still strumming over the strings of the guitar.

"I don't know, just something you don't share. Like the fact that you can hold your own with a professional country band. It doesn't have to be something big. I'll even tell you some of my own secrets."

Jared looked up from the guitar he'd been studying. "Okay, but you go first. Tell me some more of those deep, dark secrets you are hiding behind that smile you always wear."

"First, I didn't say it would be that kind of secret. You already know most of my story anyhow. I mean more like something we don't know about each other. Like…" She searched for something insignificant to share. "I know. I hide chocolate bars around my house so that I have to look for them."

"Okay, that's just weird," Jared said. "Why

don't you put them in the kitchen like everyone else?"

"Because then I'd eat them. If I hide them
I have to make a point of looking for them. It
gives me a few moments to decide if it's really
worth the trouble."

"So it keeps you from eating chocolate?"
The corners of his lips rose in a small, knowing smirk.

"That's a secret for another time," she said,
returning his smirk. "Now it's your turn."

He leaned in, copying the way she'd leaned
in to Marjorie when they'd taped their interview for the reality show. "Every week, even
though I know I shouldn't…"

Sky leaned in closer, his lips so close she
could feel his breath against her own. For a moment she forgot what he was saying, and then
his eyes met hers and something flashed between the two of them. Her breath caught and
her lips parted. She wanted him to move closer.
She wanted him to kiss her. It wouldn't take
much. Their lips were only a few inches apart.

Jared pushed back from the table, leaving
her straining toward him. "I make a really big
homemade pizza and I eat the whole thing by
myself."

Sky leaned back and glared at him. Was he

playing her? Didn't he know he'd just made her stomach flip inside out with the anticipation of feeling his lips on hers? "Why do you do that?"

"What? I like pizza," he said, beginning to strum the guitar again. She saw his body relax, just like it had when he'd been playing it earlier. She wanted to push him and discover why he kept pulling back from her, but at the same time she didn't want to have him shut her out again.

"Where did you learn to play?" she asked. Surely this was a safe subject. "Self-taught or lessons?"

"Mom made me take lessons when I was ten. I hated them at first. But she played herself and believed if you live in Music City you should at least give it a try. At least that's what she told me. I think she thought it would help me make friends."

"And did it?" She'd heard that Jared had been close to his mom. She could picture him as a young boy playing the guitar with her. Sharing something creative like music had to build a strong bond between them. It had to have been a hard blow on him to lose a second mother. Everything she'd heard about Katie Warner had been good, even the way she'd dealt with the cancer that had taken her away from her family too early.

"I made a few. Once I started playing though, I kind of forgot the people around me."

Sky could believe that. She could see how the music had affected him. He was more relaxed. More open. "I'm glad she made you take the lessons. You clearly enjoy it."

He looked at her, that deep groove between his eyebrows telling her that he had something more on his mind than music lessons. "So, you asked me a question and now I have one for you."

"Okay," Sky said, something about the intensity of his gaze making her stomach twist into knots with apprehension. "What do you want to know?"

She'd left her whole life open with that question. What had started as a way for her to find out more about Jared had taken an unexpected turn somewhere. She just hoped that it was a detour she was prepared to take.

"You told me about your life with your grandmother and your parents, but I still don't understand how or why you would fake feeling happy if you don't. It seems a lot like lying."

"I think we all lie about how we feel at some time. Don't you? I can't say I know all of your story, but you told me about losing your mother. I know you were hurt by that, anyone would be. And I know the Warners adopted you, so I take it you lost your grandmother or she couldn't take care of you."

"She died of cancer when I was six," Jared said, his voice a solemn whisper as if he didn't want to hear the words.

Sky could see that the memory of losing her still caused him pain after all these years. "I'm lucky that I still have mine. She's a tough woman. Strong and stubborn. I'll never forget the way she just accepted us when our parents left us. She might have been faking it, but if she was, I'm sure glad that she did. I guess that's where I learned you don't have a choice about what other people in your life do. But you do have a choice about how you deal with it. I dealt with my anger at my parents by accepting my grandmother's love even though my parents had convinced me that I didn't deserve it. I guess that means I owe my attitude toward life to her."

A door slammed in the back of the bus and Sky remembered where she was.

As members of the band started appearing, Jared leaned toward her and whispered, "I'm glad she was there for you. You deserve to be happy."

There was a sadness to that statement that she didn't understand. Did he think he didn't deserve to be happy? But why? Unfortunately, it was a question that would have to wait.

As the band started to assemble around them and they pulled into the parking lot of their venue, Sky reached out for the hand that was still strumming the strings of the guitar and covered it with her own. "We all deserve to be happy, Jared. Some of us just have to work harder than others to see that."

If the concert had been amazing, the after-party thrown by the Carters' reality show at the hotel where they were all staying was even better. They'd been treated to front row seats by Mindy and Trey for the concert, but as Sky wandered through the crowd of performers and invited guests in the hotel's ballroom, she found herself blown away once more by how far her country bumpkin self had come in the world.

Both she and Jared had checked on Mindy after the concert when some of the private security had ushered them into her and Trey's dressing room. Mindy had looked tired physically but invigorated with an emotional energy at the same time. It was plain to see how much she enjoyed performing.

"Sky, come over here," someone from the band called out to her. She recognized the woman as a backup singer she'd met earlier in the evening. "I want to introduce you to my husband."

"Sky," another voice shouted over the noise of the room as she was pulled into a hug by the band member whose recommendation had gotten her there.

"Hey, Jenny, it was a great concert," Sky said, hugging her back. The woman was becoming one of the most sought out fiddle players in Nashville and after the performance tonight, Sky understood why. "I haven't gotten a chance to thank you for recommending me to Mindy."

"You are an amazing midwife. I knew she would get the best of care with you," she said.

"Jenny does say you are the best," the young woman who'd called her over earlier said. "I'm Carly and this is my husband, Zack. We just found out we're pregnant."

The whole group let out a scream of excitement mixed with congratulations. "We were hoping you would be our midwife."

Sky agreed and once again congratulated the couple. A few of the performers had picked up guitars and started to play and she turned and smiled when she saw that they'd invited Jared to join them.

As the crowd gathered around them, Sky moved to the front. She eased her phone out of her pocket and snapped a quick picture of Jared. His head was bent over the borrowed guitar as his hands changed chords and strummed the strings. Jenny joined them with her fiddle and the music changed to an upbeat song that had the crowd clapping along with the melody. An older man, white haired with spindle-thin legs, offered her his hand and the next thing Sky knew she was being swung around in a dance that took her breath away.

When the music stopped, the man bowed to her and moved back into the crowd. Laughing, she looked around the stage to see Jared walking her way. She laughed and did a twirl. This must have been what Cinderella would have felt when she'd made it to the prince's ball.

Before she could stop herself, her arms flew around his neck and she pulled him into her dance, twirling him around with her. They stopped spinning and she looked up at him, laughing as she tried to catch her breath, surprised to see him smiling. That smile. Every time she saw it her heart seemed to explode with happiness.

Pushing up on her toes, she went to press a kiss on his cheek, surprising him as he turned toward her. His lips brushed against hers and the world around them disappeared. She kissed him with an abandonment that came from too much excitement, not enough sleep and a whole lot of happiness.

Then she lost control of the kiss, giving it all up to him when his lips parted hers and the kiss went deeper. Her hands dug into his shoulders, needing to hold on to something as her legs went weak when his tongue swept across hers and her lips opened up to him.

Gone was the music that had woven itself through her just moments before. Her whole world was Jared and the feel of his lips on hers. It wasn't a sweet kiss. No, this kiss was primitive, hard and hot. When he let her go, she stumbled back, her lips feeling bruised and tender.

"What was that?" she asked as he stared at her. Looking around the room, she saw that, while they might have caught some of the crowd's attention, most everyone was gathered around where a new group of guitar players formed at the other end of the room.

"You kissed me," Jared said, his voice rough with an irritation she wasn't going to stand for.

"I let myself get a little too excited, I guess." Yes, she had instigated the kiss, but she'd planned on a quick smack on the cheek. Something fun. He'd been the one to deepen it.

"Well, I wasn't expecting it. I don't do things like this. You know that. I'm not like you," Jared said as he started to turn back to the impromptu stage set up by the group.

He was brushing her off again, just like he had the night they'd shared that dance. He was making her feel like she was unimportant, like she was the only one feeling this connection, like it was easy to walk away from her. It was the same thing her parents had done. The same thing her ex had done to her.

But she wasn't that little girl or that insecure woman anymore. She would never put up with someone ignoring her or not taking her seriously again.

"Go ahead, walk away. If you can ignore what we just shared, so can I. I'm sorry I kissed you. I won't bother you again."

She turned and walked toward the door leading out of the hotel's ballroom, glad that everyone was busy enjoying the music instead of watching her humiliate herself. If anyone had noticed the two of them kissing, they didn't seem to think there was anything unusual about it. It wasn't like the two of them were well-known among the people here.

Only she knew better. That kiss could have been the start of something special. Instead it had opened her eyes to the fact that Jared didn't want her. Oh, his body might respond to hers. That kiss, that dance they'd shared, had been proof of that. But if he couldn't admit that he wanted her, if he couldn't let go of that stubborn need for control that locked others out, she would have to be the one to let him go. And she wouldn't cry. Not now. Not ever. She'd wasted too many tears on people who didn't want her in their life when she was younger. That wasn't who she was now.

So, with her head held high, she walked out of the room and headed for the elevator that would take her to her room.

CHAPTER TEN

Jared stood outside of Sky's door and knew this wasn't a good idea. She was mad at him. And though he'd like to deny it, he understood why. She had been right. There had been more to that kiss than he was willing to admit, just like there had been more to their dance.

Leave it to Sky to call him on his bull right in the middle of a ballroom. He was in awe of the way she was willing to just put herself out there. She was so open about her feelings, while he instinctively wanted to deny that he might want something more with her.

It wasn't something new. He'd struggled with admitting he needed anyone, or anything for that matter, since he was a child. It had taken him years to believe that Katie and Jack Warner really wanted him to be their son. Looking back, he knew that had hurt them, especially his mom. But after his grandmother's death when he was only six, then being sent from one foster home to another for the next two years, he'd learned that the only person he could rely on was himself and the best way to stay safe was not to draw attention to himself.

But Sky Benton had put a dent in the armor he'd always wrapped himself in, with every flirty smile and every sassy wink she'd given him over the last few months. Now the kiss they'd just shared had blown a hole straight through that armor, right over his heart. A hole that he had no idea how to patch.

Instead of going to his own room, which would have been the safe thing to do, all he wanted to do was find Sky. Maybe if he saw her, he'd find that he'd just imagined the attraction that somehow had grown from an irritating buzz of electricity when she was around him into the scorching heat of a lightning strike during that kiss.

"What are you doing out here?" Sky's voice came from the crack in her doorway.

He'd been so busy trying to make up his mind about what to do that he hadn't noticed when her door had opened.

"I'm sorry. I didn't mean to disturb you," he said as she opened the door a little more.

"I'm a woman on her own in a hotel. The sound of someone pacing outside my door is going to disturb me." She leaned against the doorframe with her arms crossed over her chest. There was no way the cartoon character pajamas she wore should be nearly as sexy as Jared was finding them.

"I wanted to…" he started.

"Whatever it is that you are about to say had better not be another criticism. I've had it with those." Her chin went up, her eyes challenging him like a defiant child.

The truth was he didn't know what he wanted to say. Sky was everything that scared him. She threw herself into life with an abandonment he didn't feel comfortable with. He'd seen her do it the night of the party at the Carters'. While he had been happy to stay on the sidelines, she'd quickly thrown herself into the center of all those famous people and fit right in. Then she'd pulled him in with her, with that dance they'd shared. She lived without any restraints—something he didn't understand. She'd been through as much as he had in her life, yet she saw no danger in opening herself up to people.

Tonight when she'd kissed him, he felt like someone had kicked him in the chest. Part of him wanted to believe her when she said they had something special. But another part of him worried that she was throwing herself into one more thing without thinking it through. She lived for the moment while he was a planner. He liked to know what the next step would be. He needed to have control of everything around him and with Sky he had no control. That need for her took it all away and it scared him.

"I'm not going to apologize," he said, though he did owe her one. He'd been brutal in his denial of how that kiss had affected him. "I know I handled everything wrong. It's just that we are such opposites."

"What does that have to do with anything? Because we have different personalities, we can't enjoy a kiss? I've never asked you for anything more than a dance or a kiss. We're two adults who are attracted to each other. It's that simple. What is wrong with the two of us enjoying ourselves for one night?"

"What we're doing here, working with the Carters, it's important for the practice and for Legacy House. We have to be professional." And this was why Sky scared him. Any other woman could have said those words and he would have agreed with her. He'd had relationships with women through college and med school that had been short and uncomplicated.

He'd always made it plain that his priority was his education. Even the women in his life since he'd gone into practice with his dad, he'd made sure they had careers of their own that left no more room for anything more serious than an occasional date. It had been a good arrangement. And if a woman started to act like they might want more from him, he backed off. What Sky was offering him was no different from what he had offered those women.

He wasn't even surprised by that. Sky lived her life to the fullest. She made it plain by her actions that she was there for a good time. He just didn't know if being another one of her good times would be enough for him.

Yeah, Sky's way of living scared him, but what choice did he have when all he could think of with her standing there in front of him was that he'd be a fool to walk away from her.

"Nothing," he said, his mind reeling from the realization that this had been inevitable all along. Somewhere in the back of his mind, when he'd made his way to Sky's room, he'd known that kiss had changed things between the two of them forever. There was no going back to ignoring how Sky affected him. He could no longer deny that his body went on alert every time she was near him. He could continue telling her that it had been just a kiss they'd shared, but he would be lying to them both. "Maybe we should try that kiss one more time and see what happens?"

Without thinking it through or trying to figure out how this would fit into his plans, he stepped toward her. One of his hands cupped that defiant chin she'd challenged him with just moments before, while his other hand reached behind her head and pulled her toward him. Their lips met and this time, there was no mistaking the magnetic energy that drew the two of them together until he didn't know which affected him the most: his desire or hers.

Her lips parted, welcoming him inside, and the sweet taste of her filled him. His hand slid lower and he pulled her closer to him.

"Well?" she asked him when he let her go. Her smile was back and as always, it made his heart beat a little faster. Knowing that somehow he put that smile on her face made it race even more.

"Why don't you invite me inside so we can try it again?" he said.

Sky wasn't sure what had changed in Jared in the last few minutes, but she wasn't going to complain. She had no doubt that he had shownd

up at her door with just another of his apologies
on his mind. She'd wanted to break through
Jared's hard outer shell for months, her interest going from curiosity to caring when he'd
started opening up to her, to full-blown desire
once she'd seen that he had the same response
to her as she had to him.

They'd played a game of cat and mouse, her
being the cat for the most part. Some women
wouldn't be comfortable with that, but with
Jared it had been fun. But after the way he'd
reacted to their first kiss, she'd been ready to
walk away. With him now asking for an invitation inside her room, things had suddenly
taken an unexpected turn.

"Come inside," she said. She turned away
from him, not reaching for his hand. This
had to be a decision he made by himself. She
needed to know that he wanted to take this step
on his own. She didn't want to wonder later if
she had led him in there. Jared valued control
of his own life more than anything else. And
if he took that step inside her room, if he laid
her on that bed, she would give him all the control he needed.

She felt his hand on her back as he joined her
before closing the door behind them. The room
wasn't large and the king-size bed took up most

of it. Turning, she waited for him to make the first move. When his arms came around her waist, she wrapped her own around his neck, settling into his embrace. His lips touched hers, hesitant at first. Was he having second thoughts?

But when he deepened the kiss, she let all her doubts go. They stood there kissing for several minutes, his hands exploring her body with a thoroughness that was just a part of who Jared was. They moved up her body, skimming the sides of her breasts before running down her sides to cup her bottom, pulling her against the hard length of him. She arched her body until her most intimate parts slid against him.

Her nipples puckered from the cold air in the room and she realized she had somehow lost her top. When he lifted her against him, she wrapped her legs around his waist. She started to protest when he laid her on the bed and untangled her legs from him, then stopped herself.

"I want to see all of you," he said, rising back from the bed and pulling her pajama pants from her body.

Her panties came next and she felt exposed to him as he stood there in front of her, still wearing the clothes he'd worn to the concert.

Then she looked at his eyes and saw the heat there. She had never had a man look at her that way, with so much desire and need. She let herself relax into the bed as he began to remove his shirt. When his pants followed, she found it harder to keep from squirming. He was a beautiful man and the anticipation of touching all of him made it hard not to reach up and pull him down to her.

But she'd promised herself that she'd let him have control tonight. So she waited for him, all the while her body becoming more aroused by the sight of him. When he finally moved toward her, her breaths were coming quicker. She wanted to touch him. To kiss him. She wanted to take him inside of her and find the release her body craved.

"You are so beautiful," he said as he placed one knee between her legs and began to climb onto the bed. When he stopped and kissed her calf, then skimmed his tongue up to the top of that thigh, she couldn't help but squirm against him. When he parted her legs and moved between them her hips bucked up to greet him. She needed him inside her now. How could he still have so much control? Couldn't he see that he was driving her wild?

"Jared, I need…" Her voice broke off as his lips grazed one of her nipples.

"Tell me what you need," Jared murmured before his lips moved up her collarbone and behind her ear. "Tell me and I'll give it to you."

He knew what she wanted. He knew yet he held himself back from her. She started to protest but then she saw his hand tremble as it came up and pushed her hair from her face. No matter how strong his control, he was close to breaking. She could wait him out, knowing that he was reaching his limit, but why? She didn't want to play games anymore.

"I need you inside me," Sky said, the words barely out of her mouth before he was parting her legs and guiding himself inside her. Her body welcomed him as he filled her with his first thrust, but he still held himself back.

"Let go for me, Jared. Give me everything you have." As if her words had broken through all his restraints, his lips took hers in a kiss that left no doubt all his control had been abandoned. His hips thrust against her, filling her with every stroke. She wrapped her arms around his shoulders and held on as she rode out a storm of desire like she had never known.

He placed one of her legs around his waist

and she arched her body as the pleasure of this new position started to build.

Her release came over her with no notice, her body shuddering as she felt Jared's body stiffen against her before he thrust inside of her one more time.

She lay there, her body spent and empty while at the same time her heart was filled with something she couldn't recognize. Satisfaction? Oh, yes, she was definitely satisfied. She'd never felt so satisfied in her life. But that wasn't it. It was something more, something that she wasn't ready to admit. Not now. Not yet. Right then, all she wanted to do was enjoy the moment. Tomorrow would take care of itself. Didn't it always?

CHAPTER ELEVEN

SKY'S PHONE RANG and she blindly reached over to the nightstand. Pushing up in the bed, she realized two things. One, it had to be very early as the sky was just beginning to lighten. And two, Jared was gone.

"Hello," Sky said, disappointed that instead of Jared it was Mindy on the phone. She'd made plans to meet her for breakfast, but not this early.

"Hey, Sky, it's Trey. Mindy's not feeling good. I've already called Jared and he's on his way up to our room. He wanted me to call you too."

"What exactly is she feeling?" Sky asked as she hurried to slip on the clothes she'd laid out the night before.

"She was up several times last night with her stomach. She says it's only a stomach bug, but I'm not sure." The concern in the man's voice was enough to have Mindy walk out of her room while still trying to get her shoes on.

"What's the room number?" she asked as she hopped on one foot into the elevator, pulling the last shoe on.

She pushed the button to take her up. The elevator stopped on the next floor and Jared joined her.

She didn't say anything about the fact that he had left her room during the night. Had he regretted their night together? She refused to believe that. Jared had wanted her last night. Unlike the kiss she had initiated, he had been the one to come to her room. But now wasn't the time to discuss what had happened between the two of them.

"Thanks for having Trey call me," Sky said, feeling an awkwardness she wasn't familiar with. "He said she'd been sick during the night, but not much else."

"It could only be a stomach bug like she thinks or it could be something more serious. She might have to cut back on performing until after the baby is born." The elevator stopped at the penthouse floor and Jared waited for Sky to exit before following.

Trey met them at the door and took them to the bedroom, where Mindy sat in bed. Her face was pale and there were dark circles under her normally bright eyes.

"I'm feeling better," Mindy said. "I'm sure it's just a bug."

"Let Jared and Sky check you out," Trey said as he kneeled beside her.

"Okay, but I don't need both of y'all. Why don't you and Jared go get a cup of coffee?"

Sky waited for Jared to protest, but instead he handed her a satchel she hadn't seen him carrying. Opening it, she saw that there were several pairs of sterile gloves inside along with scissors, a clamp and a suction bulb. Leave it to Jared to have a bag readied in case he had to deliver an unexpected baby.

"So why don't you tell me exactly what you're feeling?" Sky asked Mindy once the men had left the room.

"It's just some cramping. My stomach is a little upset I guess. I don't think it's the baby."

"When is the last time you did a kick count?" Sky asked, as she casually placed her hand on Mindy's stomach. Sky didn't have anything to monitor contractions so she would have to do it the old-fashioned way.

"I just did one. The baby is very active. Do you think there's something wrong with them?" Mindy placed her own hand on her abdomen, whether to soothe herself or the baby inside her, Sky wasn't sure.

"I don't think so," she said, her hand remaining on Mindy's abdomen as it tightened, then after a few seconds relaxed. She hadn't grabbed her watch on her way out of her hotel room so she began to count manually in her head.

"Tell me about the pain you're feeling. Does it come and go?" Sky asked. The contraction she'd felt had only lasted a few seconds, but Mindy was only around thirty-one weeks now. She didn't need to be having any contractions.

"Just some stomach cramping, like period cramps. It's not too bad. It started last night after we went to bed."

"Any bleeding?" Sky moved her hand off Mindy's stomach.

"No. I would have called you if I'd had any bleeding," Mindy said. "Should I be worried about this?"

"Sometimes that period cramping can be short, weak contractions. It's not unusual to have them during the last trimester of your pregnancy. They're usually Braxton-Hicks. Some people call them false labor, but they actually tone your uterus and help it get ready for when you do go into labor."

"So is that what I'm having?" Mindy asked. "Is that the cramping feeling?"

"Probably. I did feel a couple contractions, but they weren't strong. But with your history of having an earlier miscarriage I'd like to have you monitored. Unfortunately, I don't have one here so we'll need to go to a local hospital."

"Can we do that? Will they let you use their equipment?" Mindy's apprehension seemed to grow with each word.

"Not like you're meaning, but you can be seen at any hospital when you are pregnant. No hospital can turn you down. But let's talk to Jared. Knoxville is a big city. He can probably contact a local obstetrician who will be willing to cover you in one of the local labor and delivery wards." Sky knew that neither Mindy nor Trey would like that idea.

"Trey's going to be upset. He'll probably cancel the rest of the tour. We only have two more concerts and they are both local."

"Let's see what's going on before y'all decide anything. If it's Braxton-Hicks and your cervix hasn't made any changes, you might manage two more concerts, though that is between you and Trey. I do think it would probably be best to rest more. Maybe cancel the after-parties?"

Mindy nodded her head in agreement. "The

party last night was fun, but I shouldn't have done all that dancing."

As if in afterthought, Mindy added, "I didn't see you or Jared on the dance floor."

"I headed to bed early while the party was still going. I'm not used to all that partying like you." It was a true statement if maybe not the whole story. Why she left and what happened afterward wasn't something she was prepared to tell anyone. She'd have to talk about it with Jared at some point. It wasn't like the two of them could ignore what happened, though, by the way he was acting, it wouldn't surprise her if Jared planned to do just that. And the fact that he had left during the night without saying anything to her still bothered her even though she knew it was probably just her insecurity that had her feeling as if he regretted the night. She'd been left one too many times for it not to bother her, even though she knew she was being oversensitive due to her history.

A knock came on the door before Trey entered the room, followed by Jared. When Sky explained that she was concerned that Mindy was having some mild contractions and wanted to have her transported to a hospital for further monitoring, Jared pulled out his phone and started calling the nearby hospitals.

It was only a few minutes before he returned. "Okay. I talked to Dr. Ward at Knoxville Medical. She knows my father and she agreed to let the hospital staff know you are coming in. She's aware of the circumstances of wanting privacy and she notified the labor and delivery staff. She speaks highly of them and assures me that they'll guard your privacy."

"Do we need to call 911? Or an ambulance?" Trey asked. He'd been pacing the whole time Jared had been on the phone.

Sky removed her hand from Mindy's abdomen. "I think if you can get us a car, it would be fine. The contractions she is having are weak and irregular right now."

Jared gave her a questioning look and she answered him with a smile. "I think Jared will agree with me that we are just doing this as a precaution."

"A car should be fine," he said. "I'll call downstairs and see if they can take care of that. I saw that they had shuttle vans available if needed."

Jared headed out the door to make the call and minutes later there was a knock on the door. Mindy scowled when she saw the wheelchair, but Jared assured her it was just another precaution.

* * *

Four hours later, the four of them were on their way back to Nashville with the assurance of Dr. Ward, as well as that of Jared and Sky, that Mindy and the baby were fine. Mindy had received a liter of IV fluid as it appeared that dehydration had been the reason for the early contractions. An exam showed she hadn't begun to dilate, and the baby's fetal heart tracing had been perfect. Once the contractions had stopped and after promising everyone that she would increase her fluid intake, Mindy had been discharged and cleared to travel.

When Trey had cornered him questioning if he should cancel the two concerts that were planned over the next two weeks, Jared had done the smart thing and recommended that he discuss it with his wife, as he had assured the man again that neither his wife nor his baby were in any danger at that time.

Jared had been in this situation before, with overprotective husbands worrying that something out of their control could happen to their wife or child. After the way Jared had lost his first mother, he understood their concerns. He knew that if it was him in that position, he would have wanted reassurances too. But he knew there were never any guarantees in life.

His mother had been in perfect health before the pregnancy and even then her pregnancy had been without complications. It wasn't until after she had delivered that things had gone bad.

"Thank you again for being here," Trey said after coming out of the large bedroom in the back of the bus, where Mindy had lain down to rest.

"I'm glad I was here, though you would have been fine with just Sky." His father had been right about it being a good thing for the two of them to work together. Sky was a good midwife and had handled everything with Mindy the same as he would have himself.

It was the change in their personal relationship that he wasn't sure about now. Last night had changed everything. Becoming involved with a coworker wasn't something that he had ever considered before. He knew it was always safer to keep your personal life separate from your professional life. He'd crossed that line last night.

Yet still, he didn't regret it. What he'd experienced with Sky was different than anything he'd ever experienced before. And if he was honest, at least to himself, he had to admit that it had been much more than just a night of sex.

Holding Sky while she slept in his arms had given him a feeling of possessiveness so strong that it scared him.

"So Mindy keeps reminding me. I know my overprotectiveness drives her up the wall, but I can't help it. I keep telling her that it's my responsibility to keep them safe." Trey scratched his head before looking back up at Jared. "You would be the same way, right? If you were married and expecting a baby?"

Thoughts of Sky pregnant with his child sprang into his mind with no warning. His imagination flared with visions of a pregnant Sky, her abdomen round with his baby. Another wave of possessiveness washed over him. Sky pregnant with his baby?

Somehow, having a wife and a baby had never seemed to fit inside his plans. He worked too much. He didn't have time for a family. He wouldn't be a good husband. There were a thousand reasons for why he didn't think he was husband or father material.

But the biggest obstacle was that he had never met anyone he wanted to share his life with. There had never been anyone that he could feel safe enough to trust his heart to. No one who he trusted enough to give up the control that ensured his life was orderly and secure. And if he had met that person, that one person who he was willing to risk his heart for, would he even have enough courage to love them knowing they could be taken away from him at any time?

"I'm sure I'd be just as protective." And that protectiveness would annoy Sky no end.

He had to stop this. He couldn't think of Sky that way. This was exactly what he'd been worried about happening just moments before. He was letting what they'd shared the night before trick his mind into thinking that they had some type of future. It had only been the two of them sharing a night together. They'd both agreed to that. Hadn't they?

And even if they hadn't, the two of them couldn't be more incompatible. Sky with her live-life-in-the-moment lifestyle and his obsessive need to make decisions in a practical manner would never work together.

He thought about the night before, how she'd given up all her control to him. He would have thought that would be hard for her, but she'd seemed to enjoy it. It made him wonder how it would feel to switch roles and let Sky take control. Thinking about her being in control of him in the bedroom sparked an interest he didn't need to explore. It had taken all his strength to leave her bed the night before, he couldn't allow himself to think of picking up where they had left off. Like she had said, they were adults and it had been only for the one night.

"She's asleep," Sky said, joining the two of them at the gathering room on the bus.

The rest of their group had been sent home earlier along with the reality show's production crew. Only a couple of the Carters' trusted bandmates had been informed of why Jared and Sky were staying behind and traveling back to Nashville with Mindy and Trey. And the people who had been informed knew that Trey did not want any of this shared with any of the production crew.

"She's worried that Joe and Marjorie are going to be mad when they hear she went to the hospital without informing them," Sky said as she took a chair beside him.

"She's right, but if we'd told them they probably would have wanted to have a crew there in the hospital recording it all for the show. I wish I'd never let Marjorie talk me into doing the show," Trey said as he pulled his phone out and headed to the front of the bus to place his call.

"I think Mindy is regretting it too, but what are they supposed to do? They signed the contract. According to Mindy they're stuck in it for another two years." Sky yawned and closed her eyes. "Hopefully something more interesting will happen to take all the show's concentration off of the pregnancy. I don't understand why Marjorie is pushing the focus on the pregnancy so much. She obviously cares about them."

"We still have an hour and a half till we get home. Go take a nap in one of the bunks. Maybe if we all get lucky, Marjorie will find something else to concentrate all her attention on."

"I hope so too," she said as she headed to the back of the bus to one of the curtained bunks, "just as long as it isn't us."

CHAPTER TWELVE

Sky had to drag herself into the office Monday morning. She didn't know how Mindy did it with the late-night parties and all the traveling. After getting home Sunday afternoon, she'd barely finished the laundry she'd left for the weekend, before she was crawling into bed. She guessed the glamorous life of musicians came with a cost. Just like being a midwife came with her being on call the next twenty-four hours.

"Good morning," she called to the receptionist, stopping to see if there were any messages from any of her patients.

"Good morning. I see you had a good weekend," Leo said, handing her a couple notes. "Lori said for me to have you call her as soon as you came in."

Lori had been on for the weekend midwifery coverage at the hospital and would want to give a report on any of Sky's patients she had seen.

"I'll give her a call. Anything else I need to know?"

"Nope. What about you? Anything you'd like to share?" Leo moved in closer over his desk. "You know I can keep a secret."

Leo could keep a secret about as well as she could give up chocolate. "Nope. No secrets today."

Besides, the only secret that anyone at the office would be interested in concerned her and Jared, and that wasn't anything she planned on sharing with anyone...well, except maybe Lori.

She put her bag away and put on the white lab coat she wore around the office before glancing down at the messages Leo had taken for her. One was the message to call Lori. The other was a message from Jasmine asking her to call.

The call had been left with their answering service before the office had opened, which meant that the girl had been up early, probably getting ready for her classes. Sky put in the call but didn't get an answer. Jasmine had probably already started her classes for the day and couldn't answer.

Next she returned Lori's call. "Hey, what's up?"

"Where are you?" Lori asked, her words fast and breathless.

"I just got to the office. Why didn't you call my cell?" Sky asked, taking a seat at her desk. By the sound of Lori's voice, she knew something was wrong.

"I did call your cell. It goes straight to voicemail." Now Lori's words were clipped and sharp. Her best friend wasn't happy with her.

Sky pulled the phone out of her pocket and realized it was turned off. "Sorry. Just tell me what's up."

"Me? Why don't you tell me what's up? I wasn't off in Knoxville partying and I definitely wasn't making out with Jared."

Sky's stomach did a bounce, a twist, and then dove down to her toes as her heart rate did its own dangerous dip. "How do you know about that?"

Sky was sure Jared hadn't told anyone and she would have sworn no one had been paying attention to them at the party. But unless Lori had developed some new psychic abilities, someone had talked. She held her phone up and waited as it powered up then signaled that she had three missed calls and six text messages, most of them from Lori.

"Because ever since the office found out that Mindy has become one of our patients, the staff has been following the Carters' reality show on social media. Check your phone. I sent you the picture someone sent me."

Sky scrolled past a message from Mindy to the first message she had received from Lori this morning. A picture appeared on her screen and she recognized the room. It was the ballroom at the hotel. Trey Carter stood over to the side facing the camera with his arm around Mindy's waist. In front of him with their backs turned to the camera, some of the band members were playing. Sky could recognize Jenny from this view, but not the other players. But it wasn't the famous music stars who had been circled in red marker on the picture. From the angle of the camera, you could see two people in the background. It was unmistakably her and Jared tangled together in a kiss. That was what had been circled. That was what most of the staff had seen?

"Can we talk about it later? Maybe lunch?" Sky needed to make a call to Jared to warn him before his father saw the picture. And then she needed to have a talk with a certain receptionist who she was sure had sent the picture out to the staff.

Her phone beeped with a call from Jared. Someone must have already shown him the picture. While normally she'd be able to look at it as a reminder of a magical night she'd always treasure, she knew that this would upset him. He'd kept his life so private until they'd started working for the Carters.

And his father? He'd trusted them to represent the practice.

"I have to take another call. I'll call you back to get a report on the weekend."

She clicked over to Jared's call. "Hey. I'm sorry. I'll explain to your father that it's all my fault."

"Sky, I'm glad I got you. I'm over at the hospital. One of your patients, Khiana Johnson, just came in and it looks like she is having a placental abruption. They're taking her back to the operating room now, but I thought you might want to come over. I've got to go. I need to scrub up now." He hung up the phone and for a moment she just stared at it before she realized what he had been saying.

Khiana Johnson was a single mom and a nurse who worked at the hospital on the surgical floor. Jared hadn't said how the baby was doing but if they had been in distress she was sure he wouldn't have stopped to make a phone call.

The hospital was just across from the office, no more than a five-minute walk. If she hurried she'd be able to slip into the OR by the time the baby was delivered. She pulled off her lab jacket, threw it on the desk and headed for the back door.

Because she was starting her call rotation she was already dressed in scrubs, which meant she didn't have to change her clothes once she'd made it up to the L & D unit. She covered her shoes and hair, then after washing her hands donned her mask. Opening the door to the OB operating room, she heard the weak cry of a baby. Jared looked over at her as he handed the baby to the nursery nurse waiting with a blanket to receive the little one. The baby looked to be around five pounds, a good weight for being at only thirty-five weeks gestation, but the little boy was pale and cyanotic. Not good.

The anesthesiologist recognized her and offered her his stool beside Khiana, but she shook her head. The young mother appeared to be sleeping after receiving a dose of general anesthesia. She was in good hands. It was the baby that Khiana would want her to watch over.

"How are we doing?" she asked the pediatrician as she watched monitors being applied to the baby.

"Not bad. Usually we see this in preemies. I'm thinking his Dubowitz score will put him around thirty-five weeks gestation so he has that going for him. He's requiring some oxygen and we're getting stat labs. Just looking at his color, I suspect he's going to need a transfusion. Do you know if there was anyone here with his mom? I'll need to get consent."

"I don't. She's a floor nurse on one of the adult floors. She might have been at work. I've met her sister at one of Khiana's visits though, and I'm sure her number is in our paperwork. I'll call the office and get the number." Sky left the room feeling better now that she could at least do something to help Khiana. She wracked her brain for some missed sign that this could happen but there wasn't anything— Khiana had been in perfect health the last time she'd seen her. They'd both been happy with her weight gain and there had been no concerns for hypertension.

After calling the office, she called Khiana's sister and found out that she was already on her way to the hospital after receiving a call from Khiana's nursing manager. As soon as she hung up, her phone chimed with another call and she saw that it was Jasmine.

"Hey, Jasmine, I'm glad you called me back. What's up?"

"I'm going to tell my parents that I'm giving

the baby up for adoption today. I can't do it, Sky. I want to, for my parents, but every time I think of trying to raise the baby on my own it doesn't feel right. Maybe there's something wrong with me." The girl was becoming upset again, just like she had the day they'd talked at Legacy House.

"Take a deep breath, Jasmine. It's going to be okay. Jared told me that he could tell your mother cares about you when she came into your visits. You might disagree on what is best for you and the baby, but if you tell them what you've told me I'm sure they will support you. Give them a chance to see that you've thought this through. In the end, this is your decision, not theirs. Even if they don't understand it now, I'm sure they will come around. And until then you have a place to stay at Legacy House as long as you need it."

"Okay," Jasmine said, her voice calmer now. "Thanks for everything. I talked with your sister. She gave me the name of a local adoption agency where I can meet the people who would want to adopt the baby."

Sky gave Jasmine some more reassurance and asked her to call back after she talked to her parents. A few minutes later Jared joined her in the physician's consultation room.

"There wasn't anything I missed. Her blood pressure has been in the normal range her whole pregnancy. She doesn't smoke or do drugs. This shouldn't have happened." She'd had Leo pull up the vital signs from Khiana's last three visits and had been reassured that just like she'd remembered, there had been no issues.

"I thought I told you when I called. We know the cause of the abruption. She fell on the floor after someone spilt something and didn't clean it up. Her manager was livid."

Sky's body relaxed and she realized she'd been dreading this from the moment she'd gotten the call. She'd assumed that Jared would think it was something that she had missed. She'd hoped they were past that—working together so closely the last few weeks, he had to see that she took her patients' care as seriously as every other provider—but clearly she hadn't quite shaken off the fear that he would always view her, and possibly all midwives, as in some way less qualified, because of the circumstances of his birth mother's death.

There was nothing she could do to change that. A part of her would have even understood—an error had been made and his life had been changed forever. And still, she was surprised at the depth of her relief at hearing that he hadn't assumed she'd done something wrong with Khiana's care. His professional trust meant a lot to her.

"I'm glad you were here to take care of her. I'll go check on her before I go back to the office." She looked over to see Jared busy working on his operating report. She hated to interrupt him when he was busy. Waiting to talk to him at the office would probably be the best. Except there was no guarantee that someone wouldn't mention seeing the picture of them together before she could warn him... This might be the only chance she had.

"So, about this weekend..." Her voice trailed off. Why did this have to feel so awkward? The man had seen her naked. She should be able to talk about this without feeling so self-conscious.

"It's okay, Sky. It was one night. Like you said, we're both adults. And now that we're back to the real world, there's no reason to let it affect our professional association."

Professional association? Was he serious in thinking that nothing had changed between them?

"Look, I just need to know if anyone has

asked you about the two of us being in Knoxville with Mindy and Trey?"

"Who would know we went to Knoxville? I haven't even told my father yet," Jared said, his head still bent over the computer.

"Oh, I'd say most everyone at the office and even some of the nurses here in L & D know we were in Knoxville." There was no telling how many people had seen the picture posted on the *Carters' Way* socials. Fortunately, most would be concentrated on the stars of the show, not two lowly health care workers.

"What are you talking about?" His fingers went still on the computer and he turned in his chair so that he could see her.

"Apparently ever since it was announced that we would be taking care of Mindy during her pregnancy, most of the office has been following the reality show."

"You said you watched some of the shows. It's not surprising that some of the staff might be curious about it too. What does that have to do with us?" His shoulders shrugged and he turned back to the computer. "If they posted something about us going with them to Knoxville, it's not a big deal, though I doubt they said anything about their preterm contractions scare."

She could only beat around the bush about this for so long. It might have been easier on her if someone else had made a comment about that picture so she didn't have to be the one with news that she knew he wasn't going to like. "I don't think that was mentioned. Well, at least no one said anything about it. It's one of the pictures they posted of the two of us that's circulating through the office that has everyone's attention."

"Why? Everyone knew we would be working closely with Mindy. My father made it clear that good public relations with their reality show would be necessary. I don't see why a photo of us would be cause for much interest."

"Maybe you should see the photo. Then you'll understand." She waited for him to stop typing before she handed him her phone, where she'd pulled up the picture Lori had sent her.

He stared at the photo, not saying a word, for several moments before he handed her back the phone and turned once again to the computer without saying a word. For a second she thought about stealing the keyboard from him so he would be forced to talk to her. Then she thought of hitting him over the head with it to see if maybe that would be enough to get a human reaction out of him.

"How can you sit there and ignore this so calmly? If your father doesn't know about this already, he will soon."

"My father is not into reality shows, nor is anyone likely to have the nerve to send him the picture."

"I think we should tell him. I'll explain that it was all my fault. He knows how spontaneous I get sometimes. It might not be the kind of attention the practice needs, but except for our staff no one is going to recognize us in the background of that picture." She realized that she wasn't really worried about what other people's reaction would be to seeing her and Jared kissing. Why would she be? It wasn't like it was something she was ashamed of. It was only Jared's reaction that had worried her.

Everything between them was new and fragile. She'd convinced Jared, and almost herself, that she just wanted to have a casual relationship with him. Nothing serious. Just two adults enjoying a night together.

But after what they'd shared in Knoxville, she didn't know how that would really be enough for her now. Now she wanted time with Jared to discover if this thing between them was real. Because no matter how much she wanted to deny it, she'd fallen in love with him, something that he most definitely wasn't ready to hear. Jared was a planner and he always liked to play it safe and keep a low profile. The last thing she needed was for the two of them to come to everyone's attention, something that would be sure to have Jared running for cover. But it looked like it was too late to stop that now. All she could do was damage control.

"Telling my father isn't necessary. Like I said, it's not likely that he'll hear about this. The best thing we can do is ignore all this and not give them anything else to talk about. In a week everyone will have forgotten all about it," Jared said, his words calmly destroying all her hopes as he made it plain that was exactly what he planned to do.

So he was just going to ignore what they'd shared? Was it really possible that what had seemed so special to her had only been what she had claimed to want? Just one night for them to enjoy each other? She knew this was all her fault. She'd asked for just that one night without thinking it through. And now that she knew she wanted a chance for more, it was too late.

Without saying another word, she walked out of the room. Maybe he'd only meant they would let everyone *think* there was nothing going on between them, but she didn't think that was the case. He'd never felt comfortable getting involved with her. He saw her as someone who liked to rush into things without thinking them through.

And in this case he'd been right. She believed life was too short to measure out all the moves you made in advance. But that wasn't what this was between the two of them, she was sure of that now, because it had been building for a long time. She just hoped that Jared would see that.

She took her time getting back to the office from the hospital. The walk was mostly sidewalks and parking lots, but the spring air was soft and sweet. Spring had always been her favorite time of year. It held the promise that the cold, dark winter was over and the future held only sunshine and warmth. She used to love helping her grandmother with the planting of their garden. Then there was the waiting for those seeds to grow into the plants they would harvest. But sometimes, a late cold snap would come and freeze all the fragile ones. It always made her feel like everything she had worked for had been for nothing. Why put so much of yourself into something when you weren't going to get anything back?

That was how she felt about her relationship with Jared now. She'd tried everything to show him who she was, and to get him to let her see who he really was and what they could have together. She'd put herself out there and bared herself to him in a way she'd never done before. And for what?

She opened the back door of the office and glanced down the empty hallway, glad that everyone was busy with their patients. The last thing she wanted right now was to be questioned about her and Jared.

She'd almost made it when one of the exam rooms opened and Lori walked out followed by a very pregnant young woman with a baby on each hip.

"Megan, I promise you it won't be much longer," Lori said as she opened a door leading out to the waiting room. "I'll have the receptionist make you an appointment for next week just in case, but I suspect you'll be delivered before the weekend."

Sky had started back down the hallway when Lori caught up with her and, taking her arm, pulled her into the supply room.

"Don't think you're going to get away that

easily. Spill it, bestie. I want to know what happened in Knoxville. Don't leave out any of the details and maybe I'll forgive you for not telling me before everyone else in the office found out."

"I was going to tell you," she said, studying her hands before looking up to see one of Lori's eyebrows lift and her smile turn into a smirk that said she knew Sky wasn't telling the truth. "Okay, I don't know if I was going to tell you. I don't even know if there is anything to tell."

"I saw the picture. Why don't we start there?" Lori moved farther into the room until she came to an old exam table that had been stored in the room. Sky followed her and took a seat beside her.

"That was all my fault. The concert had been great and we were having so much fun at the party. Jared was playing with some of the band members and I was dancing with this cute old man."

"Wait. Jared was playing?" Lori asked. "Our Jared?"

"He's really good. His mom made him take lessons. He said it was so he would make friends, but I think she knew he had talent." Or maybe she was trying to give him a way to escape all the trauma he'd experienced as a child. "Anyway, it was just a spontaneous thing. He was having fun. I was having fun. I wrapped my arms around him and somehow we ended up kissing."

"And that's all it was? Just a once-and-done kiss?" Lori asked.

"Well, that was all it was supposed to be." And it would have been, except Jared had surprised her when he'd kissed her back and now there was no forgetting that kiss and the lovemaking that had followed that night. "We might have gotten a little carried away. You know how adrenaline works."

"I do. So did you tell Jared that your first kiss has now been captured for the world to see?" Lori had a wicked grin on her face. Her friend knew, just as she had, that it would be the last thing Jared would want to happen.

"I did. He seems to think as long as we ignore it, it will go away." She tried to keep the hurt from her voice.

"The attention from the kiss, or whatever it is that's happening between the two of you?" Lori asked.

Leave it to her friend to get right to the point. "I think he meant both."

They sat in silence for a moment. Sky knew she had to get to work. Her patients had been waiting too long already and she knew Lori had patients of her own to see.

She stood and stretched before heading for the door. "I wish you could see him play the guitar. It's like the music brings him out of his shell."

"I think he needs someone like you to do that. He might not know it, or at least he might not be ready to admit it, but you're good for him. He needs some fun in his life," Lori said as the two of them walked out of the supply room.

Sky went over Lori's words as she grabbed her jacket and made her way to see her first patient. She'd started out just wanting to put some fun in Jared's life with her teasing, but now she knew he deserved more. He deserved someone who would love and accept him, just the way he was. For a moment she'd thought that person might be her, but now she knew better. Because no matter what her brain tried to tell her, her heart knew she deserved to have someone accept her just the way she was just as much as Jared.

CHAPTER THIRTEEN

THERE WAS NOTHING Jared wanted more than to head home. With his day starting out with an unexpected surgery, his schedule had been thrown off from then on. The advantage of his running late was that he hadn't had time to think about Sky or the picture she'd showed him. If any of the staff were curious about it, they hadn't said anything to him. Like he'd told her, it was best just to ignore the whole thing and not give anyone else a reason to speculate about the two of them. She hadn't been happy about it, but she had to accept that he was right. He'd learned early in life that it was better to keep your head down and let people forget about you. It was safer that way when you were a foster kid who was easy prey for the bullies in the world. Without a mother or father to take up for you or protect you, becoming invisible was the only way to stay out of their way.

He'd almost made it out of the office when he heard his father's voice calling his name. He stopped and retraced his steps to his father's office.

"I thought you had gone home," he said, taking a seat in front of Jack's desk. "What are you doing here?"

"I was waiting for you to finish. I heard you started your day with an emergent C-section this morning. An abruption, Sky said." Jared's dad took off his glasses and laid them on his desk. He looked more tired than Jared felt, and that was saying a lot as Jared had barely slept since he'd come home from Knoxville.

"One of the nurses at the hospital had a fall. I just checked on the baby. He's received a transfusion and is doing well now. They expect him to get out of the NICU tomorrow if he continues without any setbacks."

"That's good," Jack said, his eyes studying his son a little too hard. "Sky told me the two of you traveled to Knoxville Saturday with the Carters and that Mindy had to be seen at the hospital there."

And what else had Sky told his father? He was afraid he knew the answer to that question. "She was a little dehydrated. She received some fluids. Nothing major."

His father's eyes still bore into him and it reminded him of the time when he was about eight and his father had questioned him about the dent in his mother's car. Jared had known that he was about to be sent back to the foster home when he'd admitted that he'd been riding his bicycle too fast on the driveway and had turned into the car to stop himself. After his dad had been assured that Jared wasn't injured, he'd sat him down and told him that he didn't need to hide things from them. If Jared messed up, his father wanted to know so he could help him make it right. It had been a turning point in their relationship. For the first time he'd felt safe in the knowledge that his parents had no intentions of sending him back into the foster system. He was their son. Forever.

"I guess Sky told you about that picture of us," Jared said. "I can explain."

"You mean the picture that I saw this morning on the *Carters' Way* show's socials?" his father asked. "No, Sky didn't say anything about it, though I gave her plenty of opportunities."

So she hadn't gone behind his back and told his father. Not that he'd had any right to ask her not to. She was involved in this as much as he was. "I asked her not to mention it. I didn't think you'd see it."

"I might not have if I hadn't overheard one of the techs chatting this morning. Do you want to talk about it?" his father asked.

Did he? It wasn't like the picture didn't explain itself. He and Sky had shared a kiss. Except it hadn't been just a kiss they'd shared. Not that he would be telling his father anything else about the night.

"I don't think so," Jared said. "I know it was very unprofessional and I'm sorry if we embarrassed you and the practice."

He started to promise his dad that it wouldn't happen again, but something held him back. No matter what he'd told Sky about the two of them, he knew there was still something between them and he didn't want to lie to his father.

"Who's embarrassed? In my day, you could kiss a girl without worrying about all the cameras people have these days. If anything, I owe you an apology for putting you in the situation. I know you value your privacy and I'm afraid you've lost some of that because of me."

"It's okay. I think you were right about me and Sky needing to work together with the Carters. You know I've had a problem with working with the midwives since they started here."

"Because of what happened with your mother. I know. It was a terrible thing to have had happen, Jared. But doctors make mistakes too. You can't hold what happened to your mother against every midwife you ever work with." They'd had this conversation a hundred times, yet it was like Jared was only now ready to hear it.

"I know. I was biased and wrong. Sky is as credible as any doctor I've worked with. We work differently, but I'm beginning to see that it doesn't have to be one or the other. Like I said, it's been good for me. I hope it's helped me grow as a doctor."

"And what about as a man?" Jack asked. "Sky's not only a competent practitioner. She's also a beautiful, strong woman."

She was all those things and more, yet still he held some part of himself back from her and he didn't even understand why. Would he ever get over being that little boy who was always too afraid to trust anyone?

"It's complicated," he said, hoping his father would let it go.

"Love's always complicated. And don't try to deny that you're in love with her. I saw the picture. That wasn't just any kiss. I'm not so old that I don't recognize the signs."

Jared started to argue with his father, then

just shook his head. Once Jack decided that he was right about something, you couldn't change his mind. Besides, Jared wasn't even sure that his father wasn't right.

For the past six months he'd told himself that he was doing his best to ignore Sky, when really he couldn't wait each day to see what outrageous thing she'd do next. He'd enjoyed every wink and every ridiculous flirty smile that she'd sent his way. Now he got up each morning looking forward not only to her smiles, but also to the time they spent working together.

"I think I'll leave now, before you get any more ideas about my love life," he said, noticing how tired his dad looked tonight. "You going to be long?"

"No, I'll be right behind you. I just want to finish this last chart of the day. Go on home."

As his dad waved him away, Jared resolved to talk to him the next day. His father had to start cutting back his time at the office. He'd worked hard building the practice and Jared knew it meant a lot to him, but it was starting to take a toll. Jared had lost too many people in his life sooner than he should have. He didn't want to lose his father too.

* * *

Sky jumped as a knock came against the door of the providers' sleep room. She couldn't complain about the interruption to her sleep. She'd only been called for one patient so far. She reached for her phone, then realized she had left it in her jacket that hung on the back of the door.

"I'm coming," she called as she rolled out of bed. The clock on the side of the bed said it was just past midnight. She couldn't have been asleep for more than an hour.

She grabbed her phone from her jacket before she opened the door. The night-shift charge nurse stood waiting for her. "What's up?"

"The emergency room just called. There's a patient on their way in by ambulance," Kelly said. "They want you down there."

"Why can't they just send the patient up here?" Sky asked as she badged herself into the unit. All obstetric patients were immediately taken up to the L & D floor unless they had a life-endangering injury.

"They didn't say, just that the emergency room doctor wanted you there when she rolled in. The report they got was the patient is pregnant and had a seizure," Kelly said as they both headed to the elevators that would take them down. "They said they weren't expecting a delivery, but I thought I'd come check out the situation."

"Thanks," Sky said as they stepped onto the elevator. The charge nurse had years more experience than Sky and more than once she'd asked the older woman for her advice with a patient.

The elevator doors opened up right in the middle of the busy emergency room. "Did they say which room they wanted me in?"

Before Kelly could answer, she recognized one of the pediatricians headed toward her as the one that had taken care of Khiana's baby.

"They called you too?" she asked, not sure why he would have been called unless they had expected a delivery.

"I was down here seeing another patient and they told me they had a pregnant seventeen-year-old coming in after having a seizure so I decided I'd stick around in case I was needed," the man said. They followed him when he turned toward the resuscitation rooms that were near the ambulance entrance.

Sky wished she had more information. She was going into this blind. If this was a real emergency then they should have called the doctor on call instead of the midwife on duty.

Her phone dinged with an incoming message and she pulled it out of her pocket. Her screen showed she'd missed three calls from the same number. And she recognized the number. Legacy House. The incoming message was from Maggie, asking her to call.

Then it hit her. Seventeen years old. Missed calls from Legacy House. And finally, a seizure that in pregnancy was usually brought on when a patient had high blood pressure and proteinuria.

She started to make a call as they reached the room only to be pushed back into the hall as a couple of EMTs came through the door with a stretcher, where Jasmine lay unresponsive and intubated.

Instead of following the stretcher into the room, Sky moved farther back from the crowd of people waiting for the patient to arrive. The phone rang twice before she heard Jared's voice. "Sky, what's up?"

She realized then that she should have waited until she had the ambulance crew's report before calling him. She needed more information to make a true diagnosis. "They just brought Jasmine into the hospital. She's had a seizure."

"I'll be right there," Jared said, before hanging up.

She knew he would be upset that he hadn't been called instead of her. Jasmine's condition was much too critical for a midwife's care, but until Jared made it there she could at least help as best she could by giving the emergency room staff the girl's background.

As the ambulance crew rolled out their empty stretcher, Sky made it inside the room. It was busy in that orderly chaotic way of emergency rooms everywhere. One nurse was applying the monitors that would give them the necessary vital signs and heart tracings while another nurse was starting an IV.

"Where's that midwife?" a young doctor called from the head of the stretcher. Sky waited as he applied his stethoscope to Jasmine's chest to check her lung sounds to make sure the ET tube was properly placed before calling out to him.

"The patient is one of my colleague Dr. Warner's patients. Jared Warner. I've called and he's on his way. I do know the patient and I can tell you that she's seventeen years old and a Gravida One, around thirty-five weeks. She's been treated for high blood pressure for the last few weeks and I know Jared was concerned about preeclampsia."

A nurse called out a blood pressure and heart rate. Both were too high.

"You need to give her a four-gram magnesium sulfate bolus, then a continual infusion of two grams per hour. Otherwise she's going to seize again." Sky turned to Kelly, who had come to stand beside her. "Find a Doppler and get fetal heart tones, then call upstairs and tell them to set up the OR for a C-section."

Kelly looked at her for a moment, then headed out of the room. Sky knew that it wasn't usual for a midwife to be the one initiating a cesarean section, but she also knew Jared wouldn't want to wait any longer than necessary to deliver the baby. Sky just prayed that the baby was okay.

She spotted a small ultrasound machine across the room. Instead of waiting for Kelly, she rolled the ultrasound over to Jasmine's side and after coating the wand with jelly, placed it on her abdomen. Taking a deep breath to prepare herself for the worst possible outcome, Sky maneuvered it till she could see Jasmine's little boy's heart. She let out her breath and her body relaxed for the first time since she'd arrived in the emergency room. She took a few screenshots for Jared, then turned to the ER doctor, who had been watching her.

"The baby's fine. Fetal heart tones look good on the ultrasound, but I want to get her on a continuous monitor." One of the baby's feet kicked out at the ultrasound wand and she laughed with relief. "I think he's ready to get out of there though."

Kelly appeared back in the doorway, the Doppler in her hand. "Sky, the patient's parents just showed up in L & D. I didn't know what you would want me to tell them."

"I wasn't sure where to send them when we picked up the patient. I guess they assumed she'd be taken up there since she's pregnant," said one of the EMTs that Sky recognized from Jasmine's arrival.

"Were her parents at Legacy House?" Sky asked. She remembered the conversation she'd had with Jasmine earlier that day. Had her parents come to the house to talk her out of going through with the adoption?

"No. She was brought in from home," the EMT said before leaving the room.

Sky needed to talk to Jasmine's parents to see what had happened and to let them know her condition, but she didn't want to leave her till Jared arrived.

"Okay, start the mag sulfate and then get her over to CT. We need to make sure her head is cleared. I want to rule out anything else going on," the ER doctor said, then nodded to Sky before leaving the room.

Though she'd seen a nurse check Jasmine for responsiveness, Sky went through the motions herself, checking Jasmine's pupils and response to pain. The minimum amount of sedation the EMTs had reported giving her to intubate could be part of the reason the girl was less responsive, or it could be that she was still postictal from the seizure.

"What happened?" Jared asked as he rushed into the room, an ER nurse behind him with the bag of magnesium sulfate Sky had requested.

"I don't know all the details, but it looks like she had a seizure. Her blood pressure when she arrived was two-twenty over one-seventeen. They're treating that, and with her history I asked them to bolus her with four grams of magnesium sulfate and then start her on two grams an hour."

Sky and Jared moved back as the nurse, having started the medication, began to roll Jasmine out of the room with the respiratory tech at her bedside assisting with the ventilator and other equipment. "They're taking her to CT now and I asked Kelly to have L & D set up for a cesarean section."

When Jared didn't say anything, Sky looked over at him to find his eyes glued to his patient. "I shouldn't have listened to her. I knew I should have admitted her last week but she got upset about being in the hospital because of her classes. She agreed to being on strict bed rest and her blood pressure reports from Maggie had been improving."

"I didn't know you'd put her on bed rest," Sky said. If Jasmine had been put on bed rest how had she been at her parents' house? Was that why the girl had called her earlier? Was she so determined to see her parents that she'd ignored Jared's orders?

"I don't understand what happened. I called Maggie on the way here and she said that when she went to give Jasmine her medications, she was gone."

None of this made sense. The last time Sky had talked to Jasmine she'd been determined to get her parents to agree with her about putting her baby up for adoption. Even though she hadn't known about the bed rest, Sky had assumed that Jasmine would call her parents on the phone or that she'd have them come see her at Legacy House.

Jared was quiet as they followed Jasmine's stretcher over to the CT department. She didn't have to ask to know that he was thinking about his mom. "This isn't your fault, Jared. I don't know everything that happened, but I do know that Jasmine left Legacy House to go see her parents."

"Why would she do that? I know she's been upset about whatever happened between her and them, but they could have come to see her."

"I don't know why she went there, but I do know…"

"Dr. Warner, the radiologist wants to see you," the charge nurse said, rushing over to them.

Sky waited while Jared and the radiologist reviewed the CT screens. Sky needed to tell him about the conversation she'd had with Jasmine and her suspicion that the young girl had gone to see her parents, hoping to get their support for her plan to find a couple to adopt her baby. But that would have to wait.

"The CT is clear. Call the ER and let them know that we are going straight up to the OB floor. I want to get her on a fetal monitor and talk to her parents," Jared said, before walking out of the room.

Unsure of what she could do to help him, Sky stayed back with Jasmine and called Kelly to see what room the charge nurse planned for them to use. Once Jasmine was taken to the pre-op area, where they were met by an anesthesiologist, Sky went to find Jared.

Jared had no problem picking Jasmine's mom out from the rest of the visitors in the waiting room, though he'd only met her a couple times. Even if he hadn't met her before he would have known Jasmine's parents anyway, because they were the only two huddled in a corner of the waiting room looking anything but excited as they waited for news of their daughter.

"Mr. and Mrs. Jameson?" he asked as he approached the couple. He'd been aware that Jasmine's parents were older than most parents of a seventeen-year-old, but the woman whose eyes met his seemed to have aged a decade since the last time he'd seen her. "Can we step out for a minute to talk?"

"Is she…is our Jasmine gone?" the woman asked him, her voice breaking with the last word.

"No. She's very sick but she's stable right now," Jared said. "What has Jasmine told you about her pregnancy?"

"Nothing, until today. She's barely talked to us since she left home. I call her every day, but she barely talks to me. She used to tell me everything…well, maybe not everything. The pregnancy was a surprise and maybe we didn't handle it as well as we should have." Jasmine's mom stopped and took a breath.

"It wasn't that we didn't support her. You know that, Lily. We told her from the first that we would help with the baby any way we could," Jasmine's father huffed, placing his arm around his wife's shoulders. "It doesn't make sense to me."

"Can you tell me what happened tonight?" Jared asked. Right now the only thing that mattered to him was the welfare of Jasmine and her baby. Everything else could be sorted out between this family later.

"Jasmine called and asked if she could come talk to us," Jasmine's mother said. "Of course I said yes. I thought she wanted to talk about coming back home. I was so excited. I offered to come pick her up but she insisted that she would take the bus."

"I thought that was why she looked so tired when she got there," the father said. "Remember, Lily? I told you that our girl didn't look good. That bus stop is three blocks from the house. She didn't have any business walking all that way."

"Actually, you are right, Mr. Jameson. I had

put Jasmine on strict bed rest due to her blood pressure being too high. She didn't tell you?"

"No, she didn't say anything about that. All she wanted to talk about was this idea that she didn't want to keep her baby. She said that she's been talking to someone in your office and she was going to help her with an adoption. We tried to make her see that she didn't need to do that. We're her parents, that baby's grandparents. She should be talking to us, not some stranger."

Why was Jared not surprised that Sky had gotten tangled up in this family's affairs?

"She said that was why she came to see us. That this woman, this midwife, told her that Jasmine had to tell us what she planned to do." Mrs. Jameson's grief had turned to anger now, something that Jared was all too familiar with.

"Like I was saying, I had put Jasmine on strict bed rest because of her blood pressure and because she was beginning to show signs of preeclampsia. From what I've been told, she had a seizure while she was at your house."

"That's right. One moment she was arguing with us and then she said she felt funny and sat down on the floor. That's when she started shaking. I didn't know what to do. Her eyes were open but it was like she wasn't there," Lily said.

"I called 911 the moment I realized what was happening. By the time they got there she wasn't shaking, but she couldn't talk to us. The EMTs said something about her airway being bad so they put a tube down her and brought her here," Jasmine's father said. "But none of this matters. What we want to know is how is she now?"

"And the baby. How is the baby?"

"Like I said, Jasmine is stable for now and the baby looks good. We've got Jasmine on some medicine to keep her from having more seizures for now and she does have a tube down her throat—more to protect her airway if she has another seizure than because she needs help breathing. Unfortunately, the only way Jasmine is going to get better is for us to take her to the operating room and deliver the baby."

He had just finished explaining to the Jamesons about the procedure and the risks to both Jasmine and the baby when he saw Sky coming toward them.

"Excuse me. I'll be back in just a moment," he said, then stepped in front of them to intercept her before she could say anything that

206 UNBUTTONING THE BACHELOR DOC

would upset the couple. The last thing he needed was for Jasmine's parents to discover that it had been Sky who had been speaking to their daughter about giving up the baby.

"Can I talk to you?" he asked her, taking her arm and leading her farther down the hall.

"Anesthesia is here and the OR is ready," she said. "Are those Jasmine's parents?"

"Yes, and you are not to go anywhere near them," he said, keeping his voice low so he wouldn't be overheard. "They said someone told their daughter that she had to tell them that she didn't want to keep the baby, and they know it was someone from our office. They're going to blame this on you. They said that she went to see them because of what you told her to do."

For a moment Sky didn't say anything. When she finally spoke, her own voice was low and her face was expressionless. "Do *you* blame me for this?"

"I know you didn't make Jasmine have a seizure," he answered, brushing his hand across his face as if he could scrub away the night. Unfortunately, it didn't work. "I just think you should have talked to me before you began advising my patient about her baby."

"You asked me to talk to her," Sky said, her voice louder now.

"If you had talked to me maybe we could have found a way to help her without her having a fight with her parents. You knew I was concerned about her blood pressure. If you'd talked to me first you would have known that Jasmine had been put on bed rest and didn't need anyone upsetting her. Didn't you know that her facing off with her parents could make her blood pressure spike?" Jared found himself getting upset and he didn't know why. "I can't even disagree with her parents—it might be that argument that caused the seizure."

"Let me talk to them. I'll explain that I was just trying to help their daughter."

"No. The last thing they need right now is for you to get them more upset. You've done enough for now." Jared wanted to take the words back as soon as he saw the hurt in Sky's eyes. He wanted to tell her that he didn't blame her for any of this, but deep inside, a part of him—the part that still hadn't found a way to forgive the midwife he blamed for his mother's death—wasn't sure. He knew that she never would have intentionally done anything to hurt Jasmine. Of course she wouldn't.

But Sky did have a tendency to do things

without thinking them through. That was part of the reason he hadn't trusted this thing between the two of them. He didn't want to be yet another thing she got involved with without thinking it through.

Sky looked past him to Jasmine's parents before turning her gaze back to him. "I'm sorry."

With those two words, she turned and walked away, leaving him wondering what she was apologizing for. For getting too involved with Jasmine and her parents? Or for getting involved with him?

CHAPTER FOURTEEN

SKY WANDERED IN and out of the room as the nurses prepared Jasmine to be taken to the OR. She felt helpless in doing anything for Jasmine, and just as helpless in dealing with Jared. Could he really be blaming her for what had happened to Jasmine?

Was he right?

She wasn't sure why she hadn't talked to him about Jasmine and her problem with her parents. And while she hadn't thought to tell him about her advising Jasmine to contact her parents and being honest with them about the reasons she didn't want to keep the baby, he hadn't shared with her that Jasmine had been put on bed rest either. Had they both been so tied up in their personal drama that they'd forgotten what was really important?

"We're taking her back now," Kelly said to Sky just as she was about to step into the room. The team started to push past her as they rolled

Jasmine out toward the OR. "Are you coming with us?"

Sky started to say yes, then remembered the look Jared had given her and his warning for her to stay out of things. He'd made it clear that he didn't want her in his OR. She was pretty sure he didn't want her anywhere near him.

"No," she said, turning and walking away from Jasmine before she could give in to the need to stay with her.

That wasn't her place. Jared had also made that clear. Sky needed to take care of her own patients and stay away from his. She made one more pass through the unit to make sure a patient from their practice hadn't come in while she'd been dealing with Jasmine, then decided that instead of going back to the doctors' sleep room, she'd go back to the office and get some work done. She had to do something to keep her mind busy while she waited to see if Jasmine was going to be okay.

She found herself becoming angry now, and she didn't like the feeling at all. She didn't do angry. She believed in the power of positivity, but there was nothing about any of this that was positive. How could Jared expect her to just walk away from a young girl that she had come to care for? Just because he could walk away from people didn't mean that she could do the same thing.

Because that was exactly what he had done. Hadn't he made that clear when he'd left her bed after making love to her? She'd wanted to talk to him about their relationship, but he'd seemed happy to pretend the whole night had never happened.

No matter how it hurt, it was time for her to face the fact that no matter how much Jared might have wanted her that night, he regretted becoming involved with her. Once more, she hadn't measured up to be the person that someone she cared about wanted.

And once more, she would get up, dust herself off and start living her life again. Next time she'd be more careful. Next time she'd protect her heart better.

Jared stood over Jasmine with the scalpel in his hand and forced his mind to forget how hurt Sky had looked when he'd refused to let her talk to Jasmine's parents. He had no doubt that she only meant to help the girl. It wasn't her fault that Jasmine's parents weren't listening to their daughter.

He had to put his thoughts of Sky away now. She'd been all he had thought of since the night they'd spent together. No, it went farther back than that night. He'd fought against thinking about Sky for months now, ever since that first time she'd looked at him across that crowded conference room and given him a smile that was as sexy as it was sweet. When she'd followed it up with that flirty wink of hers, part of him had known his life would never be the same. He'd been defeated even before he'd begun the fight. Only he'd never told Sky that. He'd been too afraid to let her know just how defenseless he was where she was concerned. And now he'd hurt her when she'd only tried to help him. He had to make that up to her, though he didn't know how.

But for now, he'd have to put all of that aside. Right now, all that mattered was his patient.

Jared took a breath and looked around the room, taking in the NICU team that had gathered to take Jasmine's baby as soon as it was born. Then he turned to look at the anesthesiologist, who nodded his head that he was ready. With his hand steady and his mind cleared, Jared made his first incision.

Thirty minutes later, there was a screaming baby boy being taken care of by the NICU team and the anesthesiologist was discussing whether to extubate Jasmine then, as she was showing signs of becoming more responsive, or wait until her blood pressure was more controlled and she was out of danger of having another seizure. Agreeing to err on the side of caution, the two of them decided that for now Jasmine would be left intubated and transferred to the critical care department, where she could be watched more closely.

By the time Jared had met with the Jamesons and shown them to the unit where Jasmine would stay for the next few days, it was past two in the morning. He knew he needed to head home and get what sleep he could before he had to start his day, but he wanted to let Sky know that Jasmine was improving and that her baby was perfect.

He expected to find her waiting for him on the unit, but when he couldn't find her one of the nurses informed him that she'd said she was going to the office to work on some charting. He knew immediately that she had left because of him. He'd hurt her and she'd chosen to leave instead of facing him. He had to fix this. Besides, he didn't like the thought of her over in the office alone in the middle of the night.

Checking on Jasmine once more, he made the walk across the parking lot to the clinic.

When he opened the back door, the motion light above him came on, illuminating the entryway. Passing the exam rooms, he called out to Sky, not wanting to startle her. He started to take the hallway that led to her office when he heard a sound farther down the entry hallway.

His heart sped up and he looked around to see if there was something close he could use for a weapon.

"Jared? What are you doing here?" Sky asked as she came down the hall, stopping when he put his finger against his lips and listened.

He heard the sound again, this time recognizing it as a groan. Realizing that the only room left down that hallway was his father's office, he motioned Sky behind him and made his way there.

The pair of motionless legs sticking out from behind his father's desk was the first thing he saw when the lights came on in the room. "Dad?" he called as he and Sky rushed around the desk to find his father lying on the floor, his eyes closed but his chest rising irregularly.

"Dad?" he whispered, his voice sounding more like the little scared boy he'd once been than the grown man he was now. He barely registered Sky's urgent voice speaking behind him. When his father's eyes blinked open, his own eyes filled with tears.

"I had to wait. I had to tell you," his father began, his voice weak as he grimaced with pain.

"I've called 911," Sky said, before dropping down beside him. Jared watched as she applied a stethoscope to his father's chest. "Jack, just rest. There's help on the way."

"Just want to tell you, I love you, son. From that first day…" His father's voice gave out and his eyes closed.

"His pulse is irregular and weak. There are no signs of trauma. I don't think it was a fall," Sky said as she ran her hands down Jack's legs and then up his arms before turning her attention to his head, then standing and running out of the room.

"Can you hear me, Dad?" Jared asked as he took his father's hand and squeezed. He knew he should be doing something, anything, to help him, but he was frozen by the fear of losing him.

Sky rushed back into the room with the office AED. After turning on the monitor, she didn't take the time to unbutton his father's shirt, instead she just ripped it open and began applying pads. As the cardiac rhythm began to scroll across the machine and the AED machine told them that a shock wasn't advised.

Sky squatted down in front of it and studied the rhythm. "It looks like a STEMI. See how the ST segment is higher here." Jared looked at where she pointed but found he couldn't take in the information. "Stay here with him. I'm going to open the door for the EMTs. If anything changes call out for me." With that she jumped back up and was gone down the hall.

"She's something, isn't she?" his father whispered, then cleared his throat. "She reminds me of my Katie. So full of life. You'll be a lucky man if you don't mess things up with her."

His father's face became pale and his lips tightened.

Jared was a doctor. Surely there should be something that he could do for his father besides sitting there and holding his hand, but nothing came to mind.

Minutes later, Jared heard Sky's voice directing the EMT crew to the office. Jared started to move back but his father's hand tightened on his with a strength that surprised him. "You're going to be okay, son."

His father's hand let go of his as the ambulance crew moved him over to their stretcher. Moments later they were gone, leaving packaging from the IV they'd started and debris strewn across the floor.

"I just talked to the ER doctor. He's calling in the interventional team now. We can probably meet the ambulance in the ER if we cut across the parking lot."

Jared stared at her. The last few minutes had been a nightmare for him, but Sky had remained calm and had taken care of his father while Jared had been unable to form a complete thought. All he could do was think about the other losses he'd suffered, and how he wasn't ready to lose his father too.

"Thank you," Jared said as he closed his arms around her. From the moment he'd seen his father lying helplessly on the ground, Jared had felt cold and alone. The warmth of Sky's body against his took all those feelings away. He hadn't been alone. Sky had been there for him the whole time. "I don't know what I would have done without you."

Sky sat next to Jared as they waited for the interventional cardiologist. Jack had been taken straight from the ER to the cath lab as soon as the emergency room doctor had confirmed that he was indeed having an ST-elevation myocardial infarction. The fact that Jack had lain in his office, unable to call for help for all those hours, had her worried about what damage had been done to his heart.

"How's Jasmine?" she asked Jared. He'd said very little since they'd found his father.

"I forgot to tell you. That's why I came over to the office. I wanted to let you know she's stable. They'll probably extubate her today, once they decrease her sedation medication."

"Thanks. I appreciate you letting me know." At least he was still keeping her updated on the young girl.

They stood as the doctor came into the room. The man looked almost as tired as she did, and she knew that she and Jared weren't the only ones who had been up most of the night.

"How is he?" Jared asked. He surprised her when he reached out and took her hand in his. "Can I see him?"

"He's going to be sleeping for a while. We had to keep him sedated for longer than usual, but we were able to place two stents. I'm going to have him watched in the ICU overnight, but I think he'll move out to the floor tomorrow. I know he has a busy practice, but he's going to have to slow down. I don't want him working at all for the next few weeks."

Jared assured him that he'd make sure his father abided by his orders. Once the doctor left, Sky quickly removed her hand from Jared's. Now that she knew Jack would be okay, there wasn't really a reason for her to stay with him. Still, she waited until one of the cardiac intensive care nurses came to take him back to see his father.

"We need to talk," Jared said, looking over to where the nurse waited for him. "About everything."

There had been so many things that she wanted to tell him, but in reality none of them would make a difference. Jared's actions had made it clear that it was better the two of them forget their night together. He hadn't even wanted to tell his father about the picture that had captured their kiss. He believed that if they ignored it, it would all go away. At first she had thought he'd meant the attention from the picture, but now she knew he meant whatever it was that had been happening between the two of them. And the truth was he was probably right. If he ignored it, eventually she would have to give up on him. Looking back she could see that it had always been her that wanted more from him. Even though he'd come to her room the night they were in Knoxville, it had been her kiss that had compelled him.

Not once had he ever been the one to make

the first move. In fact, if she hadn't started flirting with him all those months ago, they'd still be nothing more than colleagues who passed in the hallway. That wasn't saying that she regretted anything they'd shared recently. She was just realistic enough to know that no matter what she thought the two of them could have together, it wasn't going to happen.

So instead of responding, she gave him the best smile she could muster. The moment he disappeared down the hallway, she headed for the closest elevator. She wanted to get out of the hospital and away from the man that she had almost let break her heart. But there was one more stop she needed to make, no matter how mad it would make Jared.

She took the elevator to the surgical ICU waiting room on the next floor, where she spotted Jasmine's parents.

"Mr. and Mrs. Jameson, my name is Sky. I'm a midwife at Legacy Clinic," Sky said. "I just wanted to check and see how you are doing."

"You're the woman Jasmine was talking about. You're the one that told her she could give her baby up," Mrs. Jameson said.

Sky noticed that the poor woman was probably too tired to be angry at this point. "Jasmine told me that she didn't want to be a mother right now. She didn't feel that she was ready for the responsibility of a baby and she didn't think she could give her son everything that he deserves. I think your daughter was very brave and selfless in making that decision, but I assure you that it was *her* decision. I only encouraged her to speak openly with you about it. She just wants to do the right thing for her child. She might change her mind about what she wants tomorrow when she sees her son, but I hope if she still wants to go ahead with the adoption you will listen to her and respect her wishes. As a child who had parents that never wanted her, I wish my parents would have considered what was best for me instead of themselves. I'm sure you have always done what was best for Jasmine even over your own desires. That's all she's asking for you to do now."

Sky waited for Jasmine's parents to yell at her, or at the very least to tell her that she needed to mind her own business, but they just stood there staring at Sky like she had been speaking a foreign language.

Without saying another word, Sky left the waiting room. She didn't know if the Jamesons would even consider what she had to say, but for their daughter's and grandson's sakes, she hoped they would.

* * *

Jared paused at the door of the waiting room to look back at Sky before he let the nurse lead him to his father's room, where he found his father asleep, his respirations deep and even. He sat down beside him and waited for him to wake.

He found himself questioning the look Sky had given him before he'd left her. There was something about the way she'd looked at him before he left that made his chest hurt. The smile she'd given him had been nothing like the smile that always took his breath away. Instead this smile had been a little sad and her eyes had been empty, with none of the happiness they usually shone with. It reminded him of the smiles from his time in the foster system when he had to leave a new friend, because he knew they'd never be together again. A goodbye smile. A smile that said, *So long, it's been great while it lasted.*

Jared shook his head to clear it. His mind was just playing tricks on him. Sky wasn't leaving. As soon as his father woke up he'd go get her. And tomorrow when he came into the office she would be there waiting to torture him with one of her usual sassy smiles. Right now, he had to take care of his dad. Then he'd make time to talk to Sky. She had been right, they needed to talk about what was happening between the two of them.

"Why the face? Am I dying?"

Jared had been so tangled up in his thoughts that he hadn't noticed when his father had awakened. "No. You're going to be fine, though we are definitely going to have a talk about your work schedule."

"So if I'm not dying, what's wrong?" his father asked, clearly hoping to avoid the necessary conversation about the amount of hours he'd been working. "Is it Sky?"

"Do you just want me to say you were right again? Our working together has been good. Seeing her in action when we found you has given me even more of a reason to appreciate her work."

"I didn't put the two of you together so that you could learn to work together, son. I wanted to force you to open your eyes and see that there was a woman who's perfect for you." His father's voice held a hint of irritation and Jared saw that his heart rate had jumped up into the one-twenties.

"Calm down before the nurse comes in here and throws me out," he told his dad. "And what do you mean you didn't put us together because of work? You said that the Carters asked for the two of us."

"Mindy did ask for Sky, and her husband requested that there be a doctor following his wife closely, but they had asked for it to be me. But I knew that you would never make a move past that flirting game the two of you have been playing for the last few months if I didn't step in and force you to acknowledge your feelings for her." His father sighed, then closed his eyes. "I hoped you'd have the good sense to make a move, especially after I saw that picture of you two kissing. What is it going to take to make you see what's right there in front of you? You're a smart man. You can't believe that a woman like Sky is going to wait around forever."

Jared thought of that smile she'd given him earlier. He might have tried to deny it, but he'd known that something was off with Sky. His father was right. He'd pushed her away every time she got close. She'd come into his life and shattered that old, dirt-streaked window he'd always used to look out into the world and she'd pulled him into a world of laughter and joy where she chose to spend her own life. And now, no matter how hard he tried to board up that old window, he knew what it felt like to live outside it now. Oh, there was still a part of him that wanted to play it safe, that wanted to hide back behind that window. Looking out at the world instead of living in it was where he was comfortable. But that part had been getting smaller every minute he spent with Sky. His father had seen a future for him that he'd always denied wanting. But with Sky, that future looked possible. Or at least it could be if he hadn't messed it up beyond repair.

"Sir," the nurse began as she walked into his father's room, "I'm sorry, but I'm going to have to ask you to go. Your father needs his rest."

Jared reached over and grasped his father's hand in his. He remembered the first time his dad had shaken his hand. Jared had been so scared when his foster mother had told him that a couple was coming over to meet him. That they were looking for a little boy just like him to be their own little boy. His father's grip wasn't nearly as strong as it had been that day when he'd dropped down on his knee in front of Jared and offered the scared little boy he'd been a handshake. He had thought his father was the strongest man he'd ever met then. Now, after all those years, he still believed that.

"I'll be back later to see you," Jared said, repeating the words his father had said that day, all those years ago. And even though young Jared had not believed the man's words as he watched the strong man and the beautiful woman walk away from him, he'd hoped with everything inside of him that he was wrong. Just like he hoped now that he'd been wrong about that sad smile Sky had given him.

But when he returned to the waiting room and found it empty, he knew he'd been right. He'd hesitated too long, making excuses for why he and Sky shouldn't be together. He'd let her be the one that made every move, unable to admit that he'd wanted her from the first time she'd given him that priceless smile and that outrageous wink. He felt the same as the little boy he'd been as he'd watched his future father and mother walk away. There hadn't been anything he could have done that day. He'd had to wait there, helpless to control his own future.

But he wasn't helpless anymore. He wasn't going to wait and hope that Sky would seek him out to give him another chance. He was going to take control. He would get her back. And he would show her just how much she meant to him. He was tired of fighting against the love he felt for her. Instead, he was ready to fight *for* that love. Fight for Sky. Now he just had to figure out how.

CHAPTER FIFTEEN

As Sky drove up to Mindy and Trey's house, she felt none of the excitement that she had felt the first time she'd seen it. Maybe she was already becoming jaded by all the glitz and glamour of the country music stars' life. Maybe she was just tired. Or maybe it was the fact that Jared wasn't beside her today.

Well, at least this time Marjorie wasn't running toward her waving a mile-high stack of papers for her to sign. To be honest, the place almost looked deserted. When Mindy had called and asked her if she could do her a really big favor and come to the taping of her reality show today, Sky had wanted to say no. But who could refuse Mindy? The woman was as sweet as Sky's grandmother's cane syrup. Still, she wasn't up to smiling for any cameras today. Right now she wasn't sure if she would ever smile again.

As soon as she'd left Jared at the hospital,

she'd gone home and slept the day away. She'd hoped that after finally making the decision to walk away from him she'd wake up ready to move on. She'd even thought of maybe leaving Nashville. There were so many places she'd never seen. Now might be the perfect time to go exploring the rest of the world.

She didn't know how long she'd sat there in the driveway before a man she hadn't met before knocked on her car window. "Ma'am, are you Skylar Benton?"

The man backed up as Sky opened the door and climbed out of the car. "That's me." She didn't know what she was expected to wear today so she'd settled on a blue flowered maxi dress and a pair of strappy sandals. Sky wasn't sure whether Mindy wanted her to actually be on the show or be there only for moral support as she explained to the show's viewers the reason for her hospital visit.

"They're waiting for you down at the barn," the man said before tipping his cowboy hat at her, turning and walking down a path along the side of the house.

"Mindy's in the barn?" Sky asked, confused. Where was everybody? Something about this didn't feel right. She felt like the heroine in one of those horror flicks being led to her demise.

"She's around there somewhere," the man said without turning around.

Sky had never been in Mindy's backyard and upon following him along the side of the house she was surprised to see that what the man was calling "a barn" wasn't the horse barn she had been expecting. Instead, it was a pretty cedar building half the size of the house, with old-fashioned Dutch doors. She could smell fresh cut hay before she made it to the opened half door, but there were none of the usual smells of horses. A huge chandelier suspended off a thick cedar beam that ran the length of the building. Other, smaller chandeliers had been hung throughout the space, bathing it in a golden light.

Then she saw him in the middle of the large open room sitting on a stack of hay. He'd traded his spotless white lab coat for a pair of faded jeans and a chambray buttoned-up shirt. He looked like a ranch hand who'd come in from work and decided to sit awhile. Sky's heart stuttered and her breath caught in her chest when he looked up at her and began to play the guitar in his hands.

She didn't see the man who'd led her there pull open the barn door. She'd made it halfway across the room before she'd even realized it.

What was she doing? She'd made the decision to walk away from this man. He'd made it plain that he didn't want her. Not like she wanted him. He hadn't been willing to give the two of them a real chance, though time after time she'd all but thrown herself at him.

She started to turn around, to leave before he could see the tears in her eyes. She didn't cry. Not anymore. She shed enough tears when her parents had left her and when the man she'd thought had loved her deserted her. The only tears she ever allowed herself nowadays were happy tears. So why was she crying now?

Then she recognized the song he played. It was an old Alabama song. A love song about falling in love. Then Jared began to sing, "How do you fall in love? When do you say 'I do'?"

His voice wasn't trained and he'd never be a country music star, but to her it was the most beautiful song she had ever heard. By the time he got to the end, she'd given up holding back the tears. Still, when he laid the guitar down and walked toward her, his arms held out, she couldn't move. She'd gone to him over and over. She'd flirted. She'd teased. She'd opened up to him and worked so hard to get his attention and still he'd fought against what she knew they could have together. If he wanted her, he had to say the words.

As if he'd heard her prayer to heaven, he stopped in front of her and took her hands in his. "I love you, Sky. I know I've been saying that the two of us are too different, but I think those differences are what make us perfect for each other. I need the sunshine and happiness that you've brought to my life and sometimes you need me to bring you down to earth. And no matter our differences, I can promise you that for the rest of my life, I'll always love you. Will you marry me?"

"Yes," she whispered, afraid to break the spell from Jared's song.

Then he brushed her tears from her face and with his hands on her cheeks, he kissed her. It was a sweet kiss, full of a love she had feared she'd never have. But when Jared's hands slid down to her waist, pulling her closer and deepening the kiss, the barn suddenly echoed with applause.

Pulling away, Sky turned to see the whole camera crew from Mindy and Trey's reality show. Beside them stood Mindy, looking as guilty as sin, and Marjorie looking as happy as if she'd won a CMA Award.

For a moment she was afraid this had all

been just a performance for the show, but when Jared's arms slid around her, she relaxed. He would never do something as callous as that. "I think you have some explaining to do, Dr. Warner."

"Well, we had cameras for our first dance and first kiss. It just seemed right that there should be cameras for the first time I tell you I love you," Jared said. He moved his lips down to her ear and whispered, "I had to sign a form saying that even if you walked away from me, I'd let them air the footage on the show."

"And what if I had refused to agree to this being on the show?" Sky asked, still stunned by all the trouble Jared had gone through to do this for her.

"Actually, one of those forms Marjorie had us signed covered it. They just wanted me to sign for backup since this was all my idea," Jared said before taking one of her hands in his and leading her over to the camera crew.

As he began to thank Joe and the crew, Mindy walked over to stand beside her. "Are you mad?"

"I can't believe any of this. Was this really Jared's idea?" Sky had a hard time believing that he would have ever wanted to take part in something like this, let alone that he had planned this.

"Oh, yeah, I even tried to talk him out of it. He'd have been the talk of the town if you'd walked away from him. Marjorie was hoping you'd do something dramatic like slap him across the face. Not that I thought you would do anything like that. Still, there was that chance... But he said he had to do something big to make you see he was serious."

"I guess you don't get much more serious than declaring your love on national TV," Sky said.

Once the camera crew was packed up, Jared asked Mindy and Trey if they could take a walk down to the pasture to see the horses. Holding hands as they made their way to the back of the property, Sky enjoyed the quiet of the farm after all the noise of the crowd in the barn. But there was still something they needed to clear up.

"I spoke to Jasmine's parents. They know I was the one who helped her get the information on giving her baby up for adoption."

"I know. I spoke with them too and explained that you were working with me. I also told them that you did the right think providing their daughter with information on all the options available to her."

"Thank you," she said. Having Jared's support meant everything to her.

"They assured me that they love their daughter and they only want what is best for her. And, most importantly, they're willing now to support her, no matter what choice she makes about her baby."

"I'm glad. Both Jasmine and her child deserve a chance at a good life," she said.

She knew she'd never been as happy as she was in that moment.

"I'm not sure you understand what you've done," Sky said. "Even though we're nobodies next to Mindy and Trey, we're bound to get some media attention."

"I know."

"We're really getting married," she said, stopping on the path as it all suddenly hit her now that they were alone. She could hear the note of panic in her voice. "I don't care what Marjorie offers us, they are *not* going to film any part of our wedding."

"Of course not," he said, his voice a little too calm. "I've already talked to her. She has no interest in filming the wedding."

"Oh, good," Sky said, starting back down the path.

"All she wants is to film the bachelor party. I declined that one also."

She looked over at Jared, who was smiling. "What that woman needs is a man of her own."

"Don't look at me, I'm taken," he said, squeezing her hand before raising it to his lips. He stopped as they came to the fence where they could see three horses galloping across a field. Still holding her hand, he held up a beautiful gold ring with a trio of diamonds, the one in the middle larger than the other two. He'd planned everything out so perfectly for her.

"Yes, you are," Sky said, as he slid the ring on her finger. "For now and forever. You're mine."

EPILOGUE

"JUST ONE MORE big push, Mindy. The baby's crowning. Just one more and you'll finally get to hold your baby," Sky said as Jared reached over her and wiped the sweat that had formed on her forehead.

"You can do it," Trey said, helping his wife get into position for that last push.

As Mindy took in a breath and began to push, Jared handed Sky a surgical towel to use to wrap around the baby. Carefully, she helped guide the baby out, first its head and then one shoulder after the other, until she held the new little baby who would soon be the talk of Music City.

"It's a boy!" Trey yelled as he hugged his wife, who had begun to cry the moment the baby began to cry.

"With a voice like that, I bet he'll be following in his parents' footsteps," Jared said as he handed Sky the instruments to clamp the baby's cord, then handed Trey the scissors to cut the cord.

"Here's your baby boy," Sky said, reaching across Mindy and handing her the baby.

While the nursery nurse began to help the new mother, Sky stood and turned to Jared. "I'm really going to miss us working together like this."

"Who knows? Maybe Mindy and Trey will have another one," he said, smiling down at her. "What I think you're going to miss is all the media attention."

"Speaking of which," Trey said as he moved to stand beside them. "I'm supposed to tell you that Marjorie has a camera ready to record all of us together so that we can announce the birth."

A few hours later, Sky found herself straightening the collar of Jared's lab coat. As always it was spotless and pressed to perfection. While he might have become a little more relaxed in his life since she had moved in with him, there were some things that would never change.

She'd been surprised about how well he'd taken the attention his proposal had gotten. As soon as it had aired, there'd been comments on the show's media accounts ranging from kind and sweet to some suggesting that her fiancé shouldn't quit his day job. He'd taken them all with good humor, along with the ribbing by the staff at the hospital.

But today would finally be their last time in front of the cameras. Something, no matter what Jared thought, Sky was glad of. Living a life of privacy with him was much more fun than being the center of attention. Not that the two of them would be the center of attention today. Today all the attention would be on Mindy and Trey.

"You ready?" Jared asked her as they made their way to Mindy's hospital room. "You know, if you find yourself missing the limelight, Marjorie might let you come back as a special guest on the show."

"The only person that's going to be recording me after today is the wedding photographer," Sky said as they made their way through the crowd in the hallway that had gathered to see the taping of the season finale of *Carters' Way*.

Sky and Jared followed Joe's direction as he placed the two of them behind the chair where Mindy sat holding her new baby boy. Trey sat beside her, his smile just as big as it had been the moment Sky had first shown him his son.

When Jared reached for her hand, Sky smiled

and looked over at him. His eyes caught hers and to her amazement, and right in front of the cameras for all the viewers to see, he winked.

* * * * *

*Look out for the next story in the
Nashville Midwives trilogy*

Coming soon!

*And if you enjoyed this story, check out
these other great reads from
Deanne Anders*

A Surgeon's Christmas Baby
Flight Nurse's Florida Fairy Tale
Pregnant with the Secret Prince's Babies
Florida Fling with the Single Dad

All available now!